William S.
AND THE
GREAT ESCAPE

Also by
ZILPHA KEATLEY SNYDER

William S.
AND THE
GREAT ESCAPE

Zilpha Keatley Snyder

ATHENEUM BOOKS *for* YOUNG READERS

NEW YORK LONDON TORONTO SYDNEY

ATHENEUM BOOKS FOR YOUNG READERS

An imprint of Simon & Schuster Children's Publishing Division

1230 Avenue of the Americas, New York, New York 10020

ATHENEUM BOOKS FOR YOUNG READERS is a registered trademark of Simon & Schuster, Inc.

For information about special discounts for bulk purchases, please contact Simon & Schuster Special Sales at 1-866-506-1949 or business@simonandschuster.com.

The Simon & Schuster Speakers Bureau can bring authors to your live event. For more information or to book an event, contact the Simon & Schuster Speakers Bureau at 1-866-248-3049 or visit our website at www.simonspeakers.com.

Book design by Deb Sfetsios

The text for this book is set in Centaur and Gotica Lumina.

Manufactured in the United States of America

First Edition

10 9 8 7 6 5 4 3 2 1

Library of Congress Cataloging-in-Publication Data

Snyder, Zilpha Keatley.

William S. and the great escape/ Zilpha Keatley Snyder. — 1st ed.

p.   cm.

Summary: In 1938, twelve-year-old William has already decided to leave home when his younger sister informs him that she and their brother and sister are going too, and right away, but complications arise when an acquaintance decides to "help" them.

ISBN 978-1-4169-6763-7

[1. Runaways—Fiction. 2. Brothers and sisters—Fiction. 3. Family problems—Fiction. 4. Acting—Fiction.] I. Title.

PZ7.S68522Whm 2009 [Fic]—dc22 2008010377

To two other
exceptional Williams—
My father, and another William
whose incredible plays and poems
I've always loved.

His birth certificate, if he even had one, probably just said Willy Baggett, but for most of the seventh grade he'd been signing his school papers William S. Baggett.

William S. Baggett

But that, too, would change as soon as he made his move. No more Baggett then—and good riddance.

Actually, he'd started thinking about running away almost seven years ago. That was when he'd started going to school and began to learn, among other things, that not everybody behaved like Baggetts. And not very long after that he began putting every penny he could get his hands on into what he thought of as his Getaway Fund. Well, not quite every penny. He did spend a dime, now and then, on a Saturday matinee at the Roxie Theater. Watching how your favorite movie actors could make you believe they were all those different people was one thing he'd never been able to do without.

In spite of an occasional movie, his secret stash had grown pretty fast while the Baggetts still lived in the city, where there were lots of lawns to mow and flower gardens to water and weed. And even after they had to get out of town, he'd managed to add a few coins now and then by doing odd jobs at school—carrying stuff for teachers, and mopping up on rainy days for Mr. Jenkins, the janitor.

He'd made other plans and preparations too. Besides saving his earnings, he began to keep a long, narrow knapsack beside his bed, and all his most important belongings right there within arm's reach, ready to push into it. And then, someday, he would take his Getaway Fund out of its supersecret, hard-to-reach hiding place, sling his knapsack over his shoulder, and simply walk away. And that would be that.

But what then? Where would he run to? Over the years he'd changed his mind a lot, but just recently he'd come up with some interesting possibilities. Like, how about Hollywood? Or Broadway in New York City? Or even better, Stratford-upon-Avon. Okay, not likely. But, **"𝔚e are such stuff as dreams are made on."** Right?

He never told anyone, of course. Not even Jancy, at least not until after she'd pretty much guessed. But the little bit Jancy knew didn't worry him that much.

His sister would never do anything to ruin his future career. He was sure of that. Well, he *had* been sure anyway, until the day her guinea pig got flushed down the toilet, which not only messed up the plumbing, but apparently changed everything.

Sweetie Pie had been Jancy's pet ever since her fourth-grade teacher got tired of a health class experiment that involved feeding some guinea pigs fruits and vegetables, and some others nothing but candy and cookies. Sweetie Pie had been one of the stunted sweet-stuff pigs, and she never quite made it to normal guinea pig size. Not even after Jancy went to the trouble to clear off a stretch of cluttered, weed-grown land to plant a vegetable garden. She did manage to grow a little bit of healthy stuff for Sweetie Pie, and she would have grown a lot more if Gary and the twins hadn't decided to use her garden plot as one end of their football field.

Even though Sweetie Pie never got much bigger, she was, according to Jancy, the smartest, cutest guinea pig that ever lived. But then came the first of August, 1938, and Sweetie Pie's story came to a sad end.

William found out about it soon after it happened, when he overheard the twins snickering outside the bathroom door. What he heard them saying was how they'd managed to "get rid of that stinkin' rat, and let Buddy take the rap."

William wanted to pound on the door and yell at

them—not that that would have accomplished anything, except getting himself beaten to a pulp. Besides being extra big for fourteen-year-olds, Al and Andy were extra vicious. So William bit his lip and went looking for Jancy.

For a while he couldn't find her anywhere. Not in the room she shared with Trixie and Buddy, and not anywhere else in the big old wreck of a house. Not hiding behind any of the junkyard furniture in what might once have been a pretty nice living room, or out on the halfway collapsed veranda, either. But then, as he was checking the back hall, there she was, walking toward her room with her mop of hair hiding her face as usual. But when she saw him, she put her finger in her ear—their secret signal that asked for a talk in their private hideout.

Okay, fine. No amount of talk was going to do poor Sweetie Pie any good at that point, but William knew how Jancy must be feeling, and if talking would help, he was ready to listen. Ready and willing, even though it meant making a feverish (hay feverish, that is) trip to the barn—the huge, saggy-roofed building that sat about fifty yards from the condemned farmhouse where the Baggetts had been hanging out ever since they got more or less kicked out of downtown Crownfield.

Nowadays the barn was a kind of junkyard where all the Baggetts who were old enough to drive—not to mention the ones who drove even though they weren't old enough—had stashed the body parts of a whole lot of dead hot rods, pickup trucks, and motorcycles. Down there on the ground floor the scene was nothing but rusty carcasses, but up above the car cemetery there was a secret place that nobody seemed to know about except William and Jancy. A deserted area that must have been a hayloft back in the days when the huge old building had been a cow barn instead of a car dump.

So a moldy hayloft had become their favorite place to have a really private conversation, in spite of what it always did to William's hay fever. He didn't mind that much about the hay fever thing. Being forced to choose between being teased and tormented or having hay fever wasn't nearly the worst thing about being at the bottom of the Baggett pecking order.

On the plus side, the loft was fairly handy. All it took was a well-timed scamper across the cluttered yard to the barn door. And then a careful zigzag around and over fractured fenders and rusty radiators until you got to a narrow ladder that led up to a place where you could scrunch down behind a big pile of moldy hay and be fairly sure none of the bigger Baggetts would show up.

Up behind the haystack, in between William's sneezing and sniffing fits, he and Jancy had now and then managed to come up with the kind of plans that were necessary in order to survive as comparatively small and defenseless Baggetts. Plans like how to discourage Gary from throwing your books off the bus on the way to school, or where to hide your most precious possessions where Al and Andy couldn't get at them. So it was up there in the hayloft that William was waiting when Jancy's curly head and red, weepy eyes appeared over the edge of the loft floor.

The weepy eyes were no surprise. But what he certainly hadn't foreseen was how the conversation began. The very first words out of Jancy's mouth were, "Look here, William, I know you're getting ready to run away. You are, aren't you?"

Puzzled, William shrugged. "Well, yeah, I guess so. Sooner or later. Why?"

He was still wondering what his plans for the future had to do with the sad fate of Sweetie Pie, when Jancy cleared that up by explaining that she had decided that what happened to Sweetie Pie was the last straw.

"I'm just plain finished with being a Baggett," she told William fiercely. "So I'm going to run away too, as soon as ever I can."

William was shocked. "What are you talking about?" he said. "You're only eleven years old. A little kid like you can't just take off all by yourself."

Jancy threw up her hands. "Listen to me, William," she said. "I didn't mean all by myself. I said *too*. Like, with you. And it has to be real soon. Like maybe tomorrow. Don't you get it?"

William got it, but he didn't like it. However, he knew from experience that when Jancy really made her mind up about certain kinds of things that was pretty much it—not much use to argue. But he kept trying.

"But the problem is," he insisted, "I'm not ready yet. Look at me, Jancy. I'm just a kid." He shrugged and screwed up his face in the kind of lopsided smile that an actor uses to show he's joking—mostly joking, anyway. "Well okay, a supersmart and talented person, maybe, but still just a twelve-year-old kid." He was kidding, but not entirely. He was pretty smart, all right. No Baggett, not even the ones who put him down as a smart aleck and teacher's pet, could deny that.

And as for talented? Well, according to Miss Scott . . . But that was another story. The only story he had to come up with right now was one that would keep Jancy from running away. At least for a few more years.

"The kind of help you'd need for a successful getaway," he told her, "is somebody with a lot more than just smarts. Like, what you're going to need is some big, musclebound type guy."

Trying for a laugh—Jancy usually liked comedy—he stuck out his skinny chest and flexed invisible muscles.

No laugh. Jancy listened, squinty eyed and silent. He sighed. Even though she'd known about his running-away plan for a long time, she also knew, or should have, that he'd always seen it as something that was going to happen in the fairly distant future. And now, suddenly, it was like *right this minute?*

Things were moving way too fast. It wasn't more than an hour since the Sweetie Pie tragedy, and now Jancy was jumping the gun by announcing that she'd never been cut out to be a Baggett, and she was going to prove it by running away.

"Okay. Running away to where?" William asked. "Where you planning to go?"

Jancy raised her head and jutted her small pointed chin. "To Gold Beach," she said firmly. "I'm going to go to Gold Beach to live with our aunt Fiona."

William shook his head doubtfully. "I wouldn't count on it," he said. Fiona Hardison, their mother's sister, was a schoolteacher who lived in a little town on the northern California coast. A woman whom William and Jancy had met only once, right after their mother died, and that was four long years ago. "What makes you think Aunt Fiona would let you live with her?" William asked.

"Oh, she will," Jancy said. "She'll be so happy to get Trixie and Buddy back, she'll be glad to have you and me, too."

And that was how Jancy finally got around to mentioning an important minor detail. Not only would William and Jancy be running away together—they were going to be taking Trixie and Buddy with them.

Under the circumstances, Jancy's decision to give up on being a Baggett wasn't all that surprising. After all, she'd probably loved poor old Sweetie Pie more than any Baggett, except possibly William himself—and the two little kids, of course.

That was another thing about Jancy. She'd liked little things, the littler the better. Not that William, who was actually a year and a half older and a couple of inches taller than she was, could play that role very well. He wasn't really little, but according to popular opinion (Baggett opinion anyway), pretty much of a wimp. So maybe that's what made the difference with Jancy. William was aware that little and cute was way out ahead where Jancy was concerned, but skinny and wimpy might come in a close second.

That day in the hayloft, William's arguments got even more frantic after Jancy mentioned that her escape plan included Trixie and Buddy. "Holy Toledo, Jancy," he said, when she let that minor detail slip out. "You can't be serious. And I'll tell you right now that I am *very* serious about not helping commit a double kidnapping. You know what they do to kidnappers when they catch them. Like that guy who stole the Lindbergh baby. Zap!" He did an exaggerated quivering, stiff-limbed impression of an electric chair victim. Still no smile. He shrugged. "Anyway, I mean it. Count me out."

"But you told me——," Jancy was beginning when he interrupted.

"Okay, so I did say I was going to clear out, and I meant it. But I meant later. Like when I'm practically an adult. Like fourteen or fifteen. Not now, when I won't even be thirteen till next month. And as for you getting those two little kids all the way to Gold Beach? No way. Doing it all by yourself? I mean, look at you."

She did, and William did too. There she was, barely eleven years old, and small for her age. And at the moment—it was a blazing hot day—wearing one of Babe's outgrown sundresses. On Babe, who was fifteen, the dress had looked—well, kind of sexy, in a not very classy way. But on Jancy's skinny little stick of a body, it only made her look like the wrong end of a hard winter.

With the hay fever kicking in pretty badly, William had to stop to sneeze several times before he went on. "So I'm supposed to believe that what I'm looking at right this minute is a dangerous kidnapper who's going to nab two little kids and get them all the way to Gold Beach without getting caught? More than a hundred miles from here? And even if you managed to get that far before the police caught up with you, what makes you think Aunt Fiona would let you stay? She didn't even answer the last time you wrote to her."

"I know," Jancy said. "But she did write me two letters that were all about how awful bad she felt when Big Ed took Buddy and Trixie away. Like how she'd had them and loved them for two years and would have kept them forever if Big Ed hadn't showed up all of a sudden to take them back."

"Yeah, I *know*," William said. "I remember." What he knew, and would never forget, was that right after Buddy was born, their mother, Laura Hardison Baggett, died. Died very suddenly, leaving behind newborn Buddy and two-year-old Trixie to be taken care of by Big Ed and a bunch of Baggett teenagers. William had been eight years old at the time, and he remembered that final scene all too well. Especially when he was trying not to.

Back then Big Ed had been glad to let Aunt Fiona take Buddy and Trixie away to live with her. Let them go probably because there was no longer any Baggett left alive who was willing and able to change diapers. William had been willing to try, and he'd said so, but nobody would listen to him. So the two youngest Baggetts went to live with their mother's sister, who kept them for two years before Big Ed decided to take them back.

That happened right after he'd married Gertie, his third wife. What Big Ed told the welfare people was that he took the two little kids back because Gertie wanted to be a mother to them. As far as William could see, Gertie wasn't, and never had been, the least bit interested in being a mother to anyone. The way William figured, it was a lot more likely that President Roosevelt's new welfare plan had something to do with Big Ed's decision to have all his kids under the same roof. The New Deal plan that gave really poor families a certain amount of money for each of their children.

"Aunt Fiona probably didn't answer your letter," William told Jancy, "because she was sure that if she got them back, Big Ed would just show up and grab them away again."

"I know." Jancy hung her head so that a bunch of her thick, streaky-blond hair swung down, hiding her small face. Jancy got teased about her hair—got called Mop Head and Rabbit Tail and even worse names. Actually, William thought her curly hair was her best feature, at least when it was clean and combed, which wasn't all that often. He'd told her so before, but now he said nothing at all, and after a while she said, "I know" again, in a faint weepy voice. "But I am leaving, for absolute sure and certain, and I just can't leave the poor little things here all alone."

"Humph!" William snorted. "All alone? Not hardly.

Even with you gone, and maybe me too, that still leaves—let's see." He pretended to count on his fingers. "Seven"—he stopped to sneeze—"that leaves eight big Baggetts, if you count Gertie."

"Yeah, exactly," Jancy said. "That's exactly why I can't leave Trixie and Buddy here."

William got her point, and he couldn't help but agree, but just then another thought hit him. "I don't get it. What I don't get is why you'd *want* to bother with them. Well, Trixie maybe." He could sort of understand that. Trixie was kind of hard to resist. "But Buddy? I mean, wasn't he the one who flushed the toilet?"

Her face still hidden by her hair, Jancy nodded. "I know," she kind of gasped. And when she went on, her voice sounded wobbly. "But it wasn't his fault. Not really. Al, or else it was Andy—Buddy never can tell them apart—told him that a toilet is just the right size for a guinea pig bathtub, and when you flush, it's just like a guinea pig washing machine. It was that crummy twin's fault. I know it was awful dumb of Buddy to believe him, but he's only four years old. And who's going to tell him what else to not believe after both of us leave?"

William could tell she was crying by the sound of her voice, even though a heavy hunk of hair was hiding her face. "Crying won't do any good," he said.

But of course it did. After a few minutes of listening to her sobs and watching her skinny little shoulders shaking and quivering, he sighed and said, "Okay, okay. I'll think about it." And he meant it, even though it didn't take much thought to figure out that one reason, even the main reason, that Jancy wanted him to run away too was because she knew about—

"Oh thank you, thank you, William." Jancy interrupted his suspicious musings. And then her special talent for mind reading—at least where William was concerned— kicked in. "And it's not either because of your money," she said. "All that money in your running-away piggy bank."

William's snort was even louder. "My Getaway Fund is *not* in a piggy bank," he said.

"Well, whatever you keep it in," Jancy said quickly. "It's not because of your money. It's because you don't belong here either. You're not like the rest of them. You're not nearly as mean, and ever so much smarter and . . ."

William didn't have to listen to know the rest of what Jancy had to say. He'd heard her say it before when she wanted to get something out of him. But he also felt pretty sure that she said it because she knew it was true—at least the part about being smarter. But he still had a strong suspicion that his running-away money had a lot to do with it.

He shrugged. "Well, okay then, maybe I'm in. So what are your plans? I mean like *when*—and *how*?"

"When?" Jancy's smile, still tear wet, was wide and

beaming. "Well, as soon as ever I can. Tomorrow or else the next day, for sure." She nodded again, so hard her curly mop bounced up and down. "Not a minute later."

"Ookaaay," William drawled the word out slowly. "But then comes *how*. How are you going to do it?"

"Well," Jancy's big eyes rolled thoughtfully. "I guess I'll just . . ." Her voice trailed off to a whisper and then came slowly back. "Well, I'll just pack up all their clothes"—long pause—"and something to eat on the way, and then . . ."

"Yeah," William prompted. "And then?"

Jancy's bony little face widened into a wobbly smile. "And then you'll decide what to do. You will, won't you, William?"

William shoved to the back of his mind a lot of troublesome unanswered questions concerning such things as *how* and *when*, and the even more serious one about what Aunt Fiona's reaction might be to their unannounced arrival. He sneezed again, wiped his nose on his sleeve, sighed, and said, "Yeah. Well, sort of looks like I'll have to."

Back in the crumbling remains of what had once been a large farmhouse, the plumbing seemed to be working again, so what was left of Sweetie Pie must have moved on into the septic tank. So things were back to normal. Or, if not what most people would think of as normal, at least to "as usual." There was the "as usual" fistfight between two of the big guys on the back porch, the "as usual" screams from Gertie for Babe and Jancy to come help in the kitchen. And some of the usual roars demanding peace and quiet from Big Ed Baggett. Roars that made Little Ed stop yelling at Rudy or whichever other brother he was beating on, without cutting down much on how many punches he was throwing. Twenty-year-old Little Ed was Big Ed's first kid, and people went on calling him Little Ed, even after he got to be as big as a horse.

Also, as usual, Jancy was busy scooting around trying to get her hands on something she could feed Trixie and Buddy. As for William, he was on the floor behind the raggedy remains of what had once been a leather couch, eating a slightly raw bowlful of whatever it was Gertie was trying to cook. Something you might think of as beef stew if you were feeling optimistic.

When the bowl was empty, down to the last greasy drop, William peeked out, considering whether it might be possible to sneak into the kitchen and get a little more. In the end he decided against it. It looked like most of the Baggetts were there that evening, at least half a dozen of them. Whenever that many Baggetts crowded into a space where there wasn't room enough to have a real free-for-all, the only thing they could think of to do for entertainment was to pick out somebody to torment. And William knew who that was likely to be. Who, for instance, might get punched or kicked or swatted, or even picked up and kind of tossed around from one oversize Baggett to another.

Not being in the mood to be treated like a piece of playground equipment, William went the other way, scooting out the side door and up the stairs. And then on up the flimsy pull-down ladder that led to the dimly lit, slant-ceilinged attic that was his private living area. Not that the other Baggetts didn't know where he was. But most of the time they didn't bother him because of the dangerously decrepit ladder, and the fact that most of them were too big and awkward to squeeze through the small trap-door opening that led to the attic area.

There were other reasons too why William's space—
it could hardly be called a room—was fairly private.
Reasons that came and went with the seasons. Like, for
instance, the fact that there was no heat in winter, and a
certain amount of oozing dampness whenever it rained.
And now, in August?

In August, William's attic usually provided the kind
of heat that burned your eyes and throbbed in your ears,
and made even the palms of your hands wet with sweat.
Heat that on days like today would probably keep all
the bigger Baggetts downstairs with their cold beers and
electric fans.

William took off his shoes and most of his clothing
before he collapsed on top of the lumpy nest of old quilts
and sleeping bags that more or less served as a bed. But
not before he had arranged some necessities within arm's
reach. Things like his journal, his fountain pen, his water
jar, and 𝔇oubleday's ℭomplete 𝔚orks of 𝔚illiam 𝔖hakespeare.

Usually he spent some time on the journal first—
the journal that had been suggested by Miss Scott as a
summer project for anyone who was interested in writing
or acting. You should write not just about the things that
happened during the summer, Miss Scott had said, but
what you *felt* and *thought* about those events, using dialogue
whenever you could work it in. And then, if you were
interested in acting, you should read what you'd written
out loud—acting it out as you read. Like making your

voice soft and warm when you read the good things, and harsh and bitter when the words led in that direction. William had done quite a bit of reading-out-loud practice ever since school had let out earlier that summer.

Miss Scott. Someday, William thought he might write a really long essay on what he *thought* and *felt* about Miss Scott. All about how he had known how special she was that very first day of seventh-grade English. How she could make boring stuff like diagramming sentences into a kind of game, and even the mushiest poems sound so strong and important that you felt you might try to write one someday. That is, if you ever found someone you could feel that mushy about. And, of course, one of the most important things about Miss Scott had been 𝕾𝖍𝖆𝖐𝖊𝖘𝖕𝖊𝖆𝖗𝖊 and 𝕿𝖍𝖊 𝕿𝖊𝖒𝖕𝖊𝖘𝖙.

Besides teaching English at Crownfield Junior High, Miss Scott taught drama at the high school, where every year she put on a couple of plays, and one of them was always by 𝖂𝖎𝖑𝖑𝖎𝖆𝖒 𝕾𝖍𝖆𝖐𝖊𝖘𝖕𝖊𝖆𝖗𝖊. The actors were mostly high school students, but with a few especially talented nonstudents from elsewhere in the community. And last year, when skinny little William Baggett was only in seventh grade, Miss Scott had cast him as Ariel in the high school's production of 𝕿𝖍𝖊 𝕿𝖊𝖒𝖕𝖊𝖘𝖙.

He didn't know why. He would have asked her, except he was afraid that if she thought it over she might change her mind. Of course, most of the rehearsals were held after school, which left only a few times that she had to get him released from a class at the junior high. That never seemed to be a problem for Miss Scott. She not only managed to get William excused from his junior high classes whenever it was necessary, but she somehow understood, without him having to explain, why it *wasn't* necessary to inform his family that he was appearing in a play by 𝔚illiam 𝔖hakespeare.

That had been a big relief. William could just imagine what might have happened if any of the older Baggetts had shown up to watch a member of their family come onstage dressed in tights and a filmy tunic and sing things like, "𝔉ull fathom five thy father lies, 𝔒f his bones are coral made," while he bounded around the stage waving a wand that made all sorts of magical things seem to be happening.

So even though a lot of people said that the kid who played Ariel in last year's 𝔖hakespeare production had stolen the show—and even though there were four Baggett kids who were more or less enrolled at Crownfield High and managed to attend classes occasionally—if any Baggett had the slightest clue that William had played the part of Ariel, they never bothered to mention it when he was around.

When 𝔗he 𝔗empest was over and the school year nearly was, there had been the day when Miss Scott asked William to come to her office. He didn't think he'd done anything wrong, but he was still feeling a little bit nervous as he pushed open the office door. But there she was, sitting at her desk, with lots of her silky blond hair piled up on top of her head, and wearing a very modern dress that, on her, somehow managed to look slightly Shakespearean. And smiling in a way that let him know he could stop worrying about what he might have done wrong.

"William," she'd said, "I just want to be sure that you know how much I appreciated all your hard work this past semester. And also to tell you again how talented I think you are." She was reaching into her desk as she went on, "I have a book here that I really think you should have."

"A book?" William had asked, while in the back of his mind a few possibilities started flipping around. Possibilities like eighth-grade English grammar to help him get ready for next year. Or maybe something Crownfield eighth graders usually read in class, like *The Mill on the Floss*. But then Miss Scott was holding out this big five-pound package. A package that turned out to be Doubleday's Complete Works of William Shakespeare, illustrated by Rockwell Kent.

Thinking back to that very special day in June, William almost forgot about the heat of August as he reached over with both hands, pulled the heavy book closer, and opened it to where he'd left off—Twelfth Night, act one, scene three. Before that there'd been The Tempest, of course, which he'd known almost word for word by the time the production was over. And then there had been **A Midsummer Night's Dream**, which Miss Scott had suggested he read next. Now that he'd read it carefully, William could see why.

A Midsummer Night's Dream was easy to understand as soon as you managed to memorize which character was in love with which other character before they got love potions poured into their eyes. (Which, of course, changed everything so you had to start memorizing all over again.)

William did wonder if all the lovey-dovey scenes, and some of the magical stuff like fairies and a guy with a donkey's head, might turn off modern audiences— particularly teenage ones. But to William himself, some of the strange **Shakespearean** lines weren't all that different than things he heard all the time. For instance, when Egeus's daughter, Hermia, won't obey him, and he says, "**As she is mine, I may dispose of her.**"

Okay, that's a pretty weird thing for a father to say, but William could remember hearing Big Ed Baggett say, "You're my kid, and you'll do what I tell you or I'll knock your block off."

But that was **A Midsummer Night's Dream**, and now he was starting on **Twelfth Night**. In fact, he'd been planning to spend some time tonight finding out what the character named Sir Toby Belch was all about. Except that now, because of Jancy, he had other things to do.

Reluctantly William closed the huge book, picked it up, and, pulling out his big knapsack, slowly slid 𝔖𝔥𝔞𝔨𝔢𝔰𝔭𝔢𝔞𝔯𝔢 down to the bottom of the bag. First things first.

He looked around. Off to his left was a whole stack of books that would have to be left behind. Beat up, ragged copies mostly that various people, mainly teachers, were going to throw away, and had let him have instead because they knew how much he liked to read. Everything from Peter Rabbit to *Ivanhoe.* But his knapsack would hold only so much—so good-bye, books. Someday, when he was rich and famous, he'd buy brand-new leather-bound copies of every one of them.

Next came getting his money out of its secret hiding place, which involved going down to the part of the attic where the slanted roof was so low you had to slither on your stomach. It was a difficult and dangerous maneuver. Dangerous because there weren't any floorboards in that part of the attic, and if you didn't keep your balance on the narrow crossbeams, you would land on the lath and plaster ceiling—and probably go right through. Right through the ceiling and wind up in one of the second-floor bedrooms, along with a lot of ancient dust and plaster. And, with his luck, probably right on top of one of the biggest Baggetts. It was a pretty hair-raising possibility, particularly if it were to happen while you were carrying a heavy cloth bag in your teeth. A bag that held your lifetime savings.

But he managed to stay safely on the crossbeams, and once he was back at his makeshift bed, he made a hollow in the bedding and emptied the whole bag into it. Nineteen one-dollar bills, and a whole lot of nickels, dimes, and quarters. He'd counted it fairly recently, but just to make sure, he did it again before he put it all away, right next to **Shakespeare** in the bottom of the bag. There it went. A whole lot of hard-earned money. Thirty-one dollars and seventeen cents.

So he himself was almost ready, but that left a whole lot of things that needed to be worked on. Things that Jancy might, or might not, have thought about or prepared for. Which made at least one more meeting in the hayloft necessary, and at least another day after that to get ready. William got back into a raggedy pair of jeans and a faded T-shirt that used to belong to one of the twins and went looking for Jancy.

It took until early the next morning for William and Jancy to finally manage another meeting in the hayloft. By then William had the trip, at least the first half of it, carefully planned. Cleverly planned, if he did say so himself. "'Our remedies oft in ourselves do lie,'" he told himself, which was one of Miss Scott's favorite quotes. One that seemed to suggest that what you were inside might be worth something, no matter what family you'd been born into. For instance, straight-A brains might be good for something, even if some careless but all-powerful director, like God maybe, had cast you in the role of a Baggett. In the kind of family scene where, over the years, a good report card only got you punched out by Al and Andy for doing it just to show them up. But in this case he'd definitely thought up some remedies that were going to come in handy.

"So, I've been working on our getaway plan." William started the next morning's session as soon as Jancy joined him in the moldy hay. "I think it'll work pretty well, but there are still a couple of minor problems. Like, for instance, how and when all four of us are going to walk away from here carrying a bunch of luggage without anyone noticing. Have you thought about that?"

Jancy nodded quickly, stopped nodding, and began to shake her head. "Not very much," she said. "How are we going to do it, William?"

"Well, *I've* been thinking about it, and what I think is that we have to leave in the middle of the night. Like maybe three o'clock in the morning."

"Really?" Jancy gasped. "That early?"

"I'm afraid so. You know that during the day, any day till around midnight, this whole place is likely to be crawling with Baggetts, along with a bunch of their roughneck friends."

Jancy shrugged and nodded. She also knew, of course, that even though Big Ed Baggett and a couple of the oldest boys had sort of on-again, off-again jobs, the off days seemed to happen a lot oftener than the on ones. And as for the four Baggetts who were supposed to be going to summer school at Crownfield High, they seemed to spend more time thinking up reasons why they couldn't go than they ever spent at school. Which meant that some of them would probably be hanging around too, ready to witness and trip up any daylight escape attempts.

"So it seems to me," William continued, "that our

only chance would be to get everything packed and ready to go the night before, and then sneak out about three o'clock in the morning, when they're all pretty sure to be asleep."

Jancy nodded firmly. "Okay, we can do that, can't we? Why not?"

"Yeah, I know. It sounds simple enough, but there are a couple of problems. Like, for instance, we don't have an alarm clock. How are we going to wake up at three o'clock?"

"I thought you had one."

He nodded. "I used to. Well, I still have the clock, but the alarm part quit on me more than a year ago."

"But all last year you woke me up every day, in time to catch the school bus. How'd you do that?"

William shrugged—and sneezed violently. Here came the hay fever again. "I don't know for sure," he said. "It was like I got so used to a seven thirty alarm, I kind of grew one inside my brain." He grinned ruefully. "The only thing is, I don't know how to change the setting to three in the morning. But don't worry. I think maybe I've figured out how I can be awake at three o'clock. And once the two of us are awake, Trixie won't be any problem. Trixie wakes up if you just look at her."

"I know," Jancy agreed. "Being looked at is what Trixie likes best."

William couldn't help grinning. Trixie was a natural-born show-off. "But that still leaves old 'dead to the world' Buddy," he said.

"Yeah." Jancy saw the problem. "I didn't think about that." She knew that William had to sleepwalk Buddy to the bathroom at least once every night so he wouldn't wet the bed and get beat on by Gertie the next morning. The problem was, Buddy was the world's most determined sleeper. Once he got to sleep that was pretty much it until the next morning, no matter what else was happening— or what else he was doing besides sleeping. Getting him to the bathroom seemed pretty impossible at first, but then William found out that by pulling the chunky kid to his feet and walking behind him, kind of halfway holding him up until they got to the bathroom, they could get the job done, even though Buddy was pretty unconscious during the whole operation. Which was all very well as far as it went, but it didn't seem likely that he and Jancy could sleepwalk a mumbling, stumbling Buddy all the way to the bus stop in downtown Crownfield. Especially when they would have to be carrying all their most important belongings at the same time.

But then Jancy had a good idea. "How about that tin wagon that used to be Andy's? I think I saw it down there in the barn."

"Or maybe part of it?" William asked. "The last time I saw it, it only had three wheels."

Jancy jumped to her feet and said she was going to

see, and before very long she'd found the wagon and then, not too much later, its missing wheel. By the time she'd gotten the wheel pretty much attached to the wagon—Jancy was amazingly handy at chores like that—William had come up with some clever ideas about how they ought to use it.

"We can take the wagon out to the road and stash it in the bushes," he told Jancy. "And then tomorrow morning we'll just have to walk Buddy that far, and if he's still not awake we can dump him in the wagon and pull him the rest of the way."

Jancy clapped her hands and then kept them together, the tips of her fingers touching her pointed chin. "I knew you'd be able to figure out everything," she said. "Things like what time we ought to get started, and what to do about Buddy, and . . ."

She was still staring at William admiringly over the tips of her fingers when he asked, "And what?"

She sighed. And then, making it into a question, she added, "And buying our bus tickets to Gold Beach?"

"Well, maybe, maybe not." William shrugged. "Who knows how much money it takes to buy four Greyhound Bus tickets all the way to Gold Beach?"

"You don't have enough money?" Jancy's voice was quivering dangerously.

"I probably have enough," William said hastily. "You don't have to worry about that. What you do need to worry about is how we can get all the way to the station before Big Ed starts looking for us. With Buddy in the wagon or not, it's going to take us quite a while to get to Crownfield."

"Like how long do you think?" Jancy asked.

William shook his head. "Well, it's almost five miles. Five miles with two little kids and a lot of baggage. Who knows? Three or four hours?" Making a joke, he grinned and added, "Or maybe three or four days?"

At least he thought he was joking.

By the time William and Jancy climbed down from the hayloft and scooted, one at a time, across the barnyard, their planning was pretty well under way, and what each of them had to do for the rest of the day had been decided on. Jancy's assignment was to find something like suitcases or knapsacks or, if it came to that, old flour sacks. Anything that would hold her clothes as well as Buddy's and Trixie's, including jackets and shoes and some other pretty bulky stuff.

Since William already had all his stuff packed and ready to go, his first job was to pull the wagon across a few yards of overgrown ground without being noticed, and hide it under a big acacia bush right next to the highway. When that was accomplished, there was only one important thing left for him to do, and that was to take a long nap. That might not sound like a very important job, if you didn't stop to think about the fact that he was going to have to be wide-awake at three in the morning. The way he figured it, the only solution would be for him to nap as long as he could during the afternoon and then, when night came, simply stay up and wide-awake until three a.m. Sounds simple enough, huh? Finding a place to take a daytime nap might not sound like a very difficult assignment, unless all your choices happened to be in Baggett territory, on a hot day in August.

To begin with, the attic was out. At midday in August, William's attic hang-out might make it easy to believe in hell as an actual location, but other than that, it didn't serve any useful purpose. As a place to nap, for instance, it was definitely out of the question, unless you didn't mind winding up medium-rare. After checking to see just how bad it was, William quickly decided to look elsewhere.

At first no other possibility came to mind. The hayloft in the barn was almost as hot as the attic, plus there was the hay-fever thing. But by using patience and persistence, William finally discovered a solution to his problem.

Far back in the cow barn/car cemetery were the remains of an ancient Cadillac that had long ago lost its wheels and motor, but the body was pretty much in one piece—a body that included a backseat in fairly good condition. The glass in a couple of windows was missing, but to an imaginative person that was only another advantage. After hanging a couple of dripping-wet gunnysacks over the broken windows, William stretched out in a water-cooled Cadillac and slept until dinnertime.

After managing to get his hands on a little corned beef hash and a few slices of fried potatoes without being hassled too much by Gary and the twins, he went back to his Cadillac bedroom, rewet the gunnysacks, and slept until it was quite dark. It wasn't until after midnight, when the temperature had dropped quite a bit, that he made his way carefully and quietly to his attic hideout to gather up his belongings and stay wide-awake as he watched the hands of his no-longer-alarming clock creep silently toward three o'clock in the morning.

The noisy late-night hours crept by as usual, while the teenage Baggetts and their friends laughed and swore at the top of their lungs and tramped up and down the stairs. Around one the noise faded away to a few distant snores, and it wasn't until a good while after that, just as the hands touched twelve and three, that William started down, pulling his knapsack after him, hoping against hope that the extra weight wouldn't break the splintery rungs of the ladder and dump him and everything he owned on the floor with a noisy thump.

The rungs creaked but held together—another disaster safely avoided—and a few minutes later William was tiptoeing down the hall to the room Jancy shared with the little kids. Waking the two girls was quick and easy. All dressed except for their shoes, they were on their feet in a minute, wide-eyed and silent. Next was getting Buddy to the bathroom, which shouldn't make anyone suspicious, since everybody knew that was William's regular middle-of-the-night chore. Except that tonight, if they happened to meet someone, there might have to be an explanation of why both he and Buddy were wearing their daytime clothes.

Again their luck held, no Baggetts in the bathroom. But then came getting everyone downstairs, out the front door, across the front porch, and down the short path that led to the highway. That looked to be a much bigger production.

Deciding that turning on the light on the stairs was less dangerous than feeling their way down in complete darkness, William walked Buddy as far as the light switch before they all started downstairs. Jancy went first, staggering under the weight of William's heavy knapsack. Right behind her, Trixie carried a stuffed pillowcase under one arm and an equally fat flour sack under the other, every now and then making a soft squeaking noise like a halfway stifled scream. And in third—and fourth—place was Buddy, being supported, pushed along, and hoisted up and down by William. And every time Trixie gasped, or Buddy mumbled, or a floorboard squeaked, William felt a quiver run up his backbone as he imagined shuffling footsteps right behind him, and a loud voice demanding to know what the hell they thought they were doing.

The front door opened with an alarming squeak,

and closed with an even louder clunk, as the staggering procession made its way across the dangerously decrepit veranda, stumbled down the front steps, and shuffled slowly along the path to the highway.

Fortunately the night was cloudless, but the half-full moon gave barely enough light to distinguish the open road from the underbrush on either side. Once out on the tarmac, still warm and sticky from the day's heat, William's breath came a little easier, but not much. The Old Westbrook Highway wasn't a very busy road, especially at three o'clock in the morning, but even one passing car would be too many. It didn't seem likely that any driver catching sight of four overloaded kids staggering down the dark road at such an hour could be counted on to mind their own business and go right on by.

But even though their pace was frustratingly slow, not a single car appeared before they had covered the few yards to the big acacia bush and the red wagon's hiding place. Once there, Jancy managed to keep Buddy upright while William loaded the knapsack and the flour sack. Next came Buddy himself.

It wasn't easy. Buddy was a pretty solid four-year-old, and it took both William and Jancy to lift him onto the load and prop him up into an almost sitting position with the overstuffed pillowcase. After that it was a little easier. With William pulling, and Jancy and Trixie pushing and propping up Buddy, they started down the dark road.

They had been on their way for about an hour, and maybe for a mile or even two, when the crisis William had been expecting started to happen. At first there was only the sound—a faint hum that swiftly became a roar. A car was coming, and although it probably wasn't a Baggett, since it was coming from the wrong direction, it was still dangerous. It wouldn't be safe for them to be seen by anyone.

Grabbing Buddy and pulling him out of the wagon, and telling Jancy and Trixie to bring the wagon, William headed into the dark shadows beside the road. He didn't get far. A few steps past the edge of the pavement he ran blindly into a wall of stiff prickly bushes. Trying to support Buddy with one hand while he pushed his way into the undergrowth with the other, William only succeeded in dropping Buddy and falling on top of him. And then Buddy started to cry and William was shouting to the girls to "Get the wagon off the road and lie down flat."

The girls did what he told them to, and a few seconds later the car roared past without even slowing down. William got to his feet, brushing dirt and bits of dry leaves off himself and a loudly wailing Buddy.

It took awhile, maybe five or ten minutes, before Buddy calmed down enough to listen to their explanations. William tried first. "Hey, Buddy," he said, trying to sound cheerful and enthusiastic. "We're taking a walk—a nice, long walk. Only you get to ride in the wagon. See the nice wagon, Buddy?"

Buddy gulped, sobbed, and cried louder. And then Trixie said, "We're going back to where we used to live. Remember how good everything was at Auntie's house, Buddy? That's where we're going."

Buddy was still wailing.

It was Jancy who thought of calling it a game. "We're playing a game, Buddy," she told him. It's a game about finding our way in the dark." She leaned closer and took Buddy's face between her hands. "It's a game about walking in the dark."

Buddy gulped, swallowed hard, gulped again, and asked, "A game?"

Jancy nodded.

Buddy wiped his tearful face with both hands and looked around. "A game in the dark?" he asked.

"Yes, in the dark," Jancy said. "That makes it more fun. We have to walk a long way in the dark to find a surprise. Only you get to ride all the way there in the wagon, and then maybe you'll be the one who gets the surprise."

Buddy wiped his face again before he nodded and said, "And I get to ride in the wagon."

Jancy knew how to handle little kids. A few minutes later they were back on the road.

But there was still a long way to go.

They had walked for another mile or so—with William pulling the wagon, the girls pushing, and supporting Buddy who had gone back to sleep and was swaying limply from side to side—before it happened again. But this time the faint hum of a distant motor came from behind them—from back in the direction of the Baggett farmhouse.

Imagining a pickup truck full of angry Baggetts bearing down on them, William hastily lifted Buddy out of the wagon and staggered off the road, down a steep slope, and into the deeper darkness under a tree. Behind him the girls followed, dragging the lurching, tilting wagon. The noise built up to a menacing roar— nearer and louder, nearer and louder—and went on by. Silence—except for a three-way sigh of relief.

They had started to scramble back up the slope when William heard Jancy gasp. "What is it? What happened?" he asked.

"It's gone," Jancy wailed. "I can't find it. The wheel is gone."

There followed a general scramble up and down the slope with a now half-awake Buddy trying to help, stumbling around as he demanded over and over again, "What are we looking for, Jancy? Are we still playing the game? If I find it, do I get to keep it?"

It was William who found the wheel at last in the deep shadows under the tree, but then there was the problem of putting it back on the wagon. Fortunately, Jancy, the natural-born mechanic, had packed a screwdriver and a pair of pliers in with her underwear, so eventually the wheel was reattached and they were back on the road.

But it had all been very time-consuming. Looking to the east, William could see that the sky was changing from deep black to a shimmering silvery gray, and not far ahead they could see a scattering of lights. Morning was on its way, they had reached the outskirts of Crownfield, and the going-to-work traffic was beginning to build up.

By the time they reached the first turnoff on the outskirts of town, they had had to scramble out of sight three more times. "It's no good," Jancy said. "We're spending more time hiding than we are going toward town. What shall we do, William?"

He looked around, and came to a quick decision. "We'll turn off here," he told her. "That way we can get to town by going down Gardenia Street. It's a little longer that way, but it should be quieter. People who live on Gardenia probably don't get up as early as farmers do."

Gardenia Street was where a lot of nice houses had been built back in the good old days before the Depression. Old houses that, for the most part, had wide yards and big trees. It was a street where, just as William had predicted, not many lights were on that early in the morning.

At first their new route seemed to be working fine. The wagon moved more easily on sidewalks than on the bumpy highway shoulder, and a few streetlights were still on, making it possible now and then to actually see where they were going. Buddy was nearly awake, enough to sit up without being propped, and Jancy and Trixie were walking a few steps behind. They had been making good time for several minutes when Trixie suddenly began to squeal. One frantic squeal after another.

Dropping the wagon tongue, William whirled around in time to see something huge and black emerging from a gap in a high hedge and rushing toward Jancy and Trixie in great bounding leaps. Something inside William's head yelled at him, *Do something! Quick, do something!* He clearly heard those exact words, but nothing that told him what that something ought to be.

He had grabbed up his knapsack and was getting ready to swing it, heavy Shakespearean lump and all, and both Trixie and Buddy were gasping and squealing, when Jancy started walking toward the bulgy black monster, holding out her hands.

"Nice doggy," she was saying. "Come, nice doggy. Come."

When William's brain calmed down enough to quit telling him they were all about to be eaten alive, he could see that Jancy was right. It was only a dog, and apparently a pretty friendly one. Enormous, and in the semidarkness enough to scare anybody, but sure enough, friendly. Dropping the knapsack, William went back to join Jancy and be covered with sloppy but obviously welcoming kisses.

Trixie and Buddy had stopped squealing, and William had patted the dog's big head for quite a while, telling it what a good dog it was, when suddenly, right behind him, another voice was saying something.

"Hey," the voice said. "I know you." And then, shining a flashlight in William's face, she said, "You're Ariel."

He didn't know her. Not actually. He didn't think she had been in any of his classes at Crownfield Junior High, but even now, in the dim light, she did seem a little familiar. As if she might be someone he'd seen at school but hadn't particularly noticed. She had that kind of a face, somewhere in between pretty and not so pretty. But whoever she was, he couldn't help feeling a twinge of pride that she remembered seeing him in The Tempest.

"Yeah," he said, grinning. "I'm Ariel. At least I was. Who are you?"

"Clarice," she said. "Clarice Ogden. I'm . . ." She broke off. "Hey, wait a minute. I have to get that darn dog or he'll run away." She disappeared behind the hedge, and they could hear her voice calling, "Ursa. Ursa. You come back here. Come here right now." And a few minutes later she was back again with the big black dog, on a leash now, trotting obediently behind her.

Now that they could see he wasn't dangerous, Trixie and Buddy were delighted. They crowded around, holding out their hands to be licked and giggling. But the girl named Clarice wasn't paying any attention. Not to the kids, at least, or to what her dog was doing. It was easy to see that her mind was very much on something else. Her eyes were darting around, looking at each of them, shining her flashlight on the red wagon and their bags of belongings, and then once again at all four of them, one at a time. When her eyes finally turned back to William, they were wide and jiggly with excitement.

"You're running away," she whispered to William. "You are, aren't you?"

It took a few moments for William to manage what he hoped was a relaxed grin. "Running away?" He was trying for a surprised tone of voice—surprised, and hopefully, slightly amused. "What makes you think we're—" But right then Trixie's high-pitched little-kid voice cut in.

"Yes, yes." She was dancing up and down on her tiptoes. "We are. We are. Isn't it exciting? We're running away all the way to—"

Grabbing her by the back of her dress, William pulled her back where he could put one hand firmly over her mouth before he began again. "No, we're not. We just decided to walk into town, and we had to get an early start because of the heat and all, and . . ."

The girl named Clarice wasn't buying it. Her eyes were still jittery. "I know about you," she said. "I know you were Ariel, and your last name is Baggett, isn't it? I've heard about the Baggetts. My father said the Baggetts are the . . ." She paused, looking embarrassed. "Well, it doesn't matter what he said. But I can guess what happened. I'll bet something just happened that was so . . . so horrible that you had to escape, and you're taking your little sisters and brother because . . ." Long pause. "Maybe because they witnessed the crime and . . ."

But then a car was coming. Not far from where they were standing, a car was backing out of a driveway and turning in their direction, and Jancy was grabbing the wagon with one hand and Trixie with the other and heading for the break in the hedge. And then Clarice was grabbing William's arm and pulling him after them.

Crouched down behind the hedge, they all waited while a long, dark car picked up speed and purred by. "Okay," Clarice whispered. "Come with me. All of you. I know a good place for you to hide. Just leave the wagon right over there, sort of under the hedge. No one will see it there. That's right, bring all your stuff and follow me, and be very quiet. Come on, Ariel. You too." She pushed the knapsack into William's arms, grabbed the little kids' hands, and started off, with Ursa trotting behind her and Jancy behind Ursa.

It wasn't until then that William began to realize just how much he wasn't in charge anymore. For a moment he tried to stand his ground. "Wait a minute," he tried to say. "We have to keep going. We're late already. We have to get to the bus station before . . ." But no one was listening to him. Instead they were following Clarice's flashlight as she led the way into the deeper shadows under the huge trees that surrounded a big, brown-shingled house.

Try as he might to catch up with the others, William kept stumbling, dropping his knapsack, and falling farther behind until the whole procession turned a corner and came to a stop near two short flights of stairs. One that led up toward a door with a lighted window, and another that went down into darkness. It was there that William finally caught up.

"Hey, where are you taking us?" he panted. "Come on, Jancy, kids. We have to get going."

"Shh," Clarice whispered, gesturing up toward the house. "My parents will hear you."

Lowering his voice to a loud whisper, William said, "We have to hurry. It's getting late."

"I know," she whispered back. "It's already too late to get where you're going today, isn't it? The sun is almost up. So you'd better hide down here in the basement. No one will find you here. And then tomorrow morning you won't have very much farther to go."

Jancy was tugging on William's sleeve. "She's right, William. Isn't she? Can we stay here just till tomorrow? I'm so tired."

They were all looking at him, not only Clarice and Jancy, but the little kids, too. "For a whole day?" he asked. "But what about eating? We didn't bring much food."

"Oh you don't have to worry about that," Clarice said quickly. "I'll take care of that. Come on, all of you. Follow me."

So they did—followed her and Ursa down the dark steps, through a door, and into complete darkness. And then Clarice switched on a light to reveal a large cement-floored basement, neatly lined with shelves and cupboards. There was even a kind of makeshift kitchen in one corner and, in another, a small bathroom with a toilet and shower.

"See, it's like a whole house," Clarice whispered. "We used to have a cook who lived down here."

Opening one cupboard after another, she produced a lot of blankets and three canvas camp cots. She opened some other cupboards, and went on looking.

"No luck," she said finally. "No more cots."

"That's all right," Jancy said. "Trixie and Buddy can share one. One on each end."

"He'll kick me," Trixie said.

Jancy made a shushing sound. "No, he won't," she said.

Buddy looked at William. "Yes, I will," he said firmly. But when William frowned at him, he didn't say it again.

It wasn't until the little kids and Jancy were in bed, and almost immediately fast asleep, that Clarice, with Ursa back on his leash, started up the steps that led to the door. Started, and then stopped. Crooking her finger at William, she sat down on the top step and motioned for him to sit too. He did, warily, on the other side of the big dog.

"So tell me," Clarice whispered. "What happened? Why did you have to run away?" Her eyes were jittery again—wide and sharp.

William could see what she was after. She was hoping to hear something really gruesome, like that they'd all been starved, or beaten half to death, or maybe they'd witnessed a bloody murder. Something a lot more exciting than a drowned guinea pig, that was for sure.

Peering around Ursa's big, fuzzy head, William watched how the girl named Clarice was almost breathless with anticipation, and for a moment he was really tempted. Tempted to make up a story that would knock her socks off. He could do it easily enough if he wanted to. And he knew he could tell it in a way that would make her believe every word of it. He was really good at that sort of thing. He could begin by saying . . . But then he stopped.

No. He couldn't. What if she decided to call the police? And then the police would call Big Ed. And then . . . He blinked hard, trying not to think about it. Trying to wipe out a picture of Big Ed's face when he was especially angry—fierce-eyed under twitching eyebrows, with a grin that had nothing to do with laughter. He didn't even want to imagine in that direction.

So what should he tell her? Clarice was looking at

her watch and then back at William with those sharp eyes. Probably checking to see if she had enough time to hear all the gruesome stuff she hoped he was going to tell her.

But then came a sudden 𝕾𝖍𝖆𝖐𝖊𝖘𝖕𝖊𝖆𝖗𝖊𝖆𝖓 inspiration. Taking a deep breath, he said slowly and clearly and with what Miss Scott called good projection, "'𝕿𝖍𝖊 𝖍𝖔𝖚𝖗'𝖘 𝖓𝖔𝖜 𝖈𝖔𝖒𝖊;/𝕿𝖍𝖊 𝖛𝖊𝖗𝖞 𝖒𝖎𝖓𝖚𝖙𝖊 𝖇𝖎𝖉𝖘 𝖙𝖍𝖊𝖊 𝖔𝖕𝖊 𝖙𝖍𝖎𝖓𝖊 𝖊𝖆𝖗.'"

She stared at him, and he stared right back. "What . . . what . . . ?" she was saying.

"It's from 𝕿𝖍𝖊 𝕿𝖊𝖒𝖕𝖊𝖘𝖙," he told her, grinning. "You know, the play at the high school?"

"Oh, yes. My whole English class saw it. And then I went to see it again with my parents. My parents know Miss Scott. She's an old friend of my mom's. They go to see all her plays. More than once, usually. Anyway, that's how I knew who you were. Who you were in the play, I mean."

"Oh yeah? So, anyway," William said, "what I said just then is what Prospero says to Miranda when she asks him about the storm he just magicked up." Putting back on his wise old man expression, he repeated, "'𝕿𝖍𝖊 𝖍𝖔𝖚𝖗'𝖘 𝖓𝖔𝖜 𝖈𝖔𝖒𝖊;/𝕿𝖍𝖊 𝖛𝖊𝖗𝖞 𝖒𝖎𝖓𝖚𝖙𝖊 𝖇𝖎𝖉𝖘 𝖙𝖍𝖊𝖊 𝖔𝖕𝖊 𝖙𝖍𝖎𝖓𝖊 𝖊𝖆𝖗.'"

The girl named Clarice stared at him wide-eyed for a second before she said, "Oh yeah. I guess I remember that part." She went on staring at William then, for an almost embarrassing length of time, before she sighed, shook her head like she was coming out of a trance, looked at her watch again, and said, "I have to go now."

He grinned at her. "You don't want to ope your ears?"

She pointed to her watch. "I do. I do want to hear all about everything, but my folks will be getting up soon, so I have to go now. And all of you better be very quiet for a while. After they leave for work, I'll fix you some breakfast. But be sure you all be very quiet until then."

William checked out his sleeping siblings and the one invitingly empty cot. "No problem," he said.

When he woke up out of a really sound
sleep, it took William a minute to realize
where he was—a minute of not remembering and having
a vague suspicion that he didn't want to. Keeping his eyes
and his groggy brain tightly closed down, he reached out
sneakily with one hand and felt what was around and
under him.

Definitely not his usual attic sleeping place. Not
as lumpy or smelly. Cautiously, he opened one eye and
looked around—and it all came flooding back. All of it:
The sneaking out of the house at three in the morning,
the long, scary trip down the dark road, and then being
rescued by the girl named Clarice. He sighed. Rescued—
or captured? He was climbing out of his creaky cot when
Jancy whispered, "Hi, William. I'm awake too. What
time is it?"

William shook his head. It felt late; maybe too late
to take Buddy to the bathroom. Alarming thought. He

jumped up and hurried to where Trixie was curled up at one end of their camp cot and Buddy at the other. Good news: Buddy, the cot, the blankets, and Trixie's feet were all dry.

By the time he and Buddy came out of the little bathroom, everyone was awake. Even Buddy. Awake and all talking at once. Asking questions like, "Where's my surprise, Jancy?" That was Buddy. "Where's that big dog?" from Trixie. And from Jancy a worried, "What do we do now, William?"

"Hush," William told them. "Be still until—until . . ." Grabbing his knapsack, he opened it and dug around until he found the clock that no longer alarmed. It was still ticking, however, and it said eight fifteen. They were all jabbering again when he remembered what Clarice had said about being quiet until her parents left for work, but she hadn't mentioned what time that would be. He had just begun to explain why they had to be quiet, when the door to the basement opened and Ursa bounded down the steps, followed by Clarice.

"All clear," Clarice said. "They're gone. Follow me, all of you."

So they did. As soon as everyone had their shoes on, they went up the stairs that led out of the basement, and then the other short flight that led into a big, amazingly clean kitchen, where a table was set with five plates and glasses and a big platter full of pancakes. The little kids

and Jancy were all positively bug-eyed. William tried not
to be.

Trixie was on her tiptoes checking out the shiny stove,
and Buddy was running his hands up and down the big
refrigerator.

"What's this, Willum?" he asked.

"It's like an icebox," William told him. "Only it makes
its own ice."

"Why?" Buddy demanded. "Why does it do that?"
But then he noticed the pancakes and changed the subject.
Grabbing Jancy's hand, he jerked it and pointed. "Look,
Jancy. Is that the surprise? Is that for me?"

It wasn't long before they were all seated at the table,
eating pancakes with maple syrup and drinking milk.
While the little kids were too busy eating to interrupt,
William finally got a chance to talk to Clarice.

"Look," he said. "When do your folks get home?
Won't they notice something's different? I mean, won't
they wonder what happened to all the pancakes and
milk?"

Clarice shrugged. "They won't notice anything. I
made the pancakes after they left. I'm good at making
pancakes. And I'll get some more milk before they get
home. I'll go on my bicycle and get some more milk and
some other stuff for you guys to have for dinner. It's not
far to the store. It only takes five minutes on my bike."

"Hey, that sounds great," William said. "And another

thing. Could I borrow an alarm clock for tomorrow morning? We'll have to get up real early so we can get to the bus stop before seven. We probably should leave here about six."

Clarice looked at him for a long moment before she nodded her head. "You have to leave tomorrow morning at six o'clock? Okay. I guess that will work out all right," she said, speaking slowly. Very slowly, and looking at him out of the sides of her eyes, the way you would if you were in a play, and you were supposed to give the impression that you were trying to fool somebody. He hoped he was wrong, but he'd done enough acting to know how to do that kind of a sneaky look.

A little later, when the pancakes were all gone and Jancy and William were helping wash the dishes, Trixie kept pushing the kitchen door open and peeking into the next room. When Jancy told her to stop it, Trixie ran to Clarice and said, "Do I have to? Do I have to stop peeking?" She was giving Clarice the whole Trixie treatment, with dimples and batting eyelashes. It worked.

"Come on," Clarice said. "You want to see some more of the house? Okay, if you promise not to touch anything." So of course Trixie promised, and Buddy did too. But just to be on the safe side, William whispered to Jancy to keep her eye on Trixie while he watched Buddy.

The next room was a big dining room with a long table and lots of chairs, and then there was a parlor with a fireplace and a kind of library at one end with at least a thousand books, or maybe even more. And upstairs they got to look at Clarice's bedroom and her own private bathroom, and then, best of all, something Clarice called "the playroom": a whole room full of toys. Toys on shelves and on the floor and in chests and boxes. Stuffed toys and windup toys and things that ran on a track or rocked back and forth, and some others, like large dolls, that just sat there quietly and managed to look almost alive.

Ursa, who had been trotting along with them, stopped outside the door. When Jancy held the door open for him, he stepped back, and Clarice said, "He won't come in. My folks hired a trainer to teach him not to, because he used to chew up all the stuffed toys."

William grinned. "You hear that?" he told the little kids. "No chewing on the stuffed toys." Trixie looked insulted. "Or even touching."

Trixie put her hands behind her back and walked slowly around the room. "I'm not touching," she said. "See me, Clarice? See how I'm not touching?"

Buddy did and said almost the same thing. "See me, Clice. I'm not touching too. I'm not touching more better than Trixie."

"Her name," Trixie said firmly, "is Clarice."

"That's what I said," Buddy said. "See me, Clice. See me."

But Clarice was looking at William, obviously waiting for a comment. "Not bad," he told her, grinning.

"Just kid stuff," she said. "I hardly ever come in here anymore." She shrugged. "In fact, I never did spend much time in here. My folks thought I did, but they weren't around enough to notice."

"They weren't around much?" William said. "Where were they?"

"Working." Clarice shrugged again. "They have these big, important jobs. They're lawyers, both of them. They're very important people. Maybe you've heard of them. Jefferson and Adele Ogden, attorneys at law?"

William shook his head. He was confused, but interested. Somehow the boastful comments Clarice had made about her parents didn't fit with her sarcastic tone of voice. He was briefly curious—and might have been even more so, if he didn't have so much else on his mind. Things like how to get the little kids away from all the toys any time in the near future. "I don't know if this was a good idea," he said to Clarice. "You may never get them to go back to the basement." He motioned to where Trixie and Buddy were almost, but not quite, touching one thing after another.

"You may be right," Clarice said, nodding and smiling. Smiling in a way that reminded William of something he'd noticed before. Which was that people who weren't particularly much to look at could look a whole lot better when they smiled. She went on smiling for a moment before she said, "Okay, kids. If you go back to the basement right now, each of you can pick out one toy to take with you, as long as it's something that's not too breakable."

Great joy and excitement, and a few minutes later they were all on their way downstairs, with Trixie clutching a Shirley Temple doll in a pink dress, and Buddy a tin clown that turned somersaults when you wound him up.

On their way through the kitchen, Clarice got a bunch of stuff out of the refrigerator and bread box and told William and Jancy they should take it down to the basement and make some sandwiches when it was lunchtime. "The stove down there doesn't work anymore," she said. "But there are some dishes and knives and forks and like that in the cupboards. You'll have to make your own lunch, because I'll be gone for a while. Like maybe for two or three hours."

"It will take you two or three hours," Jancy asked, "to go shopping?"

It wasn't until then that Clarice explained that she really wasn't supposed to be home alone all day. "I'm supposed to spend most of the day with my aunt, who lives just a couple of blocks away. My folks think I spend most of every day there," she said. "But usually I don't. My aunt doesn't care. Actually, she's my great-aunt and she's pretty old, and most of the time she's reading or sleeping. She doesn't notice whether I'm there or not, except at lunchtime. So after I shop I'll have lunch with my aunt like always. I usually help make it, because my aunt's cook is giving me cooking lessons. But then I'll come right back here. Just be sure all of you stay right here in the basement until I get back. Okay?"

"What about Ursa?" Jancy asked. "Do you take him with you?"

"Not when I ride my bike," Clarice said. "He's only supposed to go outside on a leash, because he runs away. He usually just stays in the house while I'm gone, but you can keep him down here with you in the basement if you want to, until I get back."

Jancy did want to. "But can I take him out so he won't mess on the floor?" she asked.

Clarice shook her head. "No. Don't take him outside. You won't need to. He's used to waiting all day. The only time he has to go in a hurry is sometimes real early in the morning. That's how come I happened to find you guys this morning. Ursa woke me up and absolutely insisted that he had to go out right then, even though it was still pretty dark outside." She thought for a moment and then went on. "Maybe he heard you. Maybe that's why he wanted to go so early."

So it turned out that it was only because the dog named Ursa wanted to go outside early in the morning that the runaway Baggetts wound up spending the next day at the Ogdens'. Except for the fact that he was anxious to get the running-away ordeal over and done with, William wasn't too upset about the delay. Not at that point, anyway.

The trip to the bus stop would be a lot easier tomorrow. There was enough bread and cheese and apples to make a pretty good lunch, and the little kids had the doll and the tin clown to play with for the rest of the day. Nothing to worry about—you might think.

You might also think that an expensive doll with eyes that opened and shut, and a tin clown that turned somersaults, would be enough to keep a six- and a four-year-old fairly happy for a few hours. They weren't, though, and that was how it happened that William started doing 𝕿𝖍𝖊 𝕿𝖊𝖒𝖕𝖊𝖘𝖙 in the Ogdens' basement.

It didn't happen right away. For the next hour or so, while the little kids played with their borrowed toys and Jancy played with Ursa, William got his **Complete Works** out of his knapsack. He started where he'd left off: act one, scene three of **Twelfth Night**, and it was pretty interesting. All about how Olivia's uncle, Sir Toby Belch, stayed out late and drank too much and had good-for-nothing friends. Probably a Baggett ancestor, William decided.

But it wasn't easy to keep his mind on what he was reading with all the other things that were going on in the basement. Jancy was talking to Ursa, Trixie was talking to the Shirley Temple doll and pretending to be the doll talking back to her, and the tin clown kept clanking up and down the cement floor. After a while, William gave up on **Shakespeare** for the time being and asked Jancy to help him make lunch. Making and eating the cheese sandwiches didn't take long, and then William was back to trying to ignore everything except **Shakespeare**.

But it got harder and harder to keep his mind on what he was reading. Trixie and Buddy got bored with the toys and started romping around the basement with Ursa. And when they were tired of that, they started whimpering and whining. Trixie whimpered and Buddy whined.

"Can we go play outside, Willum?" Buddy whined. And when William said no, he switched to "Why?" His all-time favorite word. William had kept count once—the score was thirty-seven whys in five minutes.

"Wow. They're driving me crazy," William told Jancy.

"Yeah, me too," she said. She tipped her head to one side and thought a moment. "Why don't you read to them?"

"Me?" William laughed. "I don't have anything to read—except **Shakespeare**."

"I know that," Jancy said. "Why don't you read Shakespeare?"

He laughed. "Read **Shakespeare** to those two? I don't think so."

Jancy nodded. "Yeah, I know," she said. "Most people couldn't. But I'll bet you could. When they don't understand, you could kind of act it out. You know, like you did in the play."

That was a shock. "How'd you find out about the play?" he demanded.

Jancy grinned. "I saw you do it. Twice. I ditched class twice and snuck over to the high school all by myself. I sat way back in the last row, but I could tell that you were a really good Ariel, and everybody thought what you did was the best part of the whole play."

William was amazed. "You never told me you saw it," he said accusingly. "Why didn't you tell me?"

Jancy looked away. She didn't say anything for several minutes, and when she did, wide-eyed and solemn, it was just, "Why didn't *you*? Why didn't *you* tell *me*?"

There were things that might have been said. Things about how afraid he'd been that the rest of the Baggetts would find out and ruin everything, but he knew that wouldn't be good enough. Finally, all he said was, "I'm sorry I didn't tell you."

Jancy grinned. "That's okay. I liked seeing it anyway. And I bet Trixie and Buddy will too."

And that was how it happened that William began to read and recite, and actually act out, parts of **The Tempest** by **William Shakespeare** in the middle of the afternoon in the basement of a brown-shingled house on Gardenia Street.

Jancy had lined everybody up—the two kids, herself, and even Ursa—like the front row of an audience. When they were all in line and quiet, William began.

"The first scene of 𝕿𝖍𝖊 𝕿𝖊𝖒𝖕𝖊𝖘𝖙," he said, "takes place on a ship, and there's this tempest. That's like a really big storm, with thunder and lightning and high winds. And everybody thinks they're going to drown. Right at first there are just these sailors running around trying to fix the sails and——"

"And right there on the stage," Jancy interrupted, "the actors who are pretending to be sailors are rocking back and forth like they're on a boat, and the big wind is blowing canvas sails and everything around all over the stage. It was real scary." She turned to William. "How'd they do that, William?" she asked. "How'd they make a big wind like that blow indoors?"

"It's a wind machine," William told her. "It's like a great big fan. Can I go on now?" They all nodded. He opened the big book to page 1299 and put it on the counter in the little kitchen, where he could remind himself what came next when he needed to. But he didn't read it word for word. Mostly he just did it the way he thought they might understand. Like, to begin with, "'𝕳𝖊𝖎𝖌𝖍 𝖒𝖞 𝖍𝖊𝖆𝖗𝖙𝖎𝖊𝖘. 𝕿𝖆𝖐𝖊 𝖎𝖓 𝖙𝖍𝖊 𝖙𝖔𝖕𝖘𝖆𝖎𝖑 𝖔𝖗 𝖜𝖊 𝖗𝖚𝖓 𝖔𝖚𝖗𝖘𝖊𝖑𝖛𝖊𝖘 𝖆𝖌𝖗𝖔𝖚𝖓𝖉.'"

He ran around then, pretending to be pulling on a rope that was taking in the sails, and leaning back and forth to make it look as if the floor was tilting under his feet. The little kids laughed and clapped.

"And now," he said, "the wind is still blowing, but

four more men come onstage, all dressed up in fancy clothes like kings and other rich people. And one of them has a beard and gray hair because he is an old man named Gonzalo. He's a good guy. Then there's a king with a crown named Alonso, and a duke, who's almost as important as a king but not quite. And the duke's name is Antonio. Remember Antonio, because he's the bad guy. The other person is named Ferdinand, and he's the king's son and he's supposed to be young and very good-looking. You got all that? Okay, action. First I'm going to be a bossy sailor called a boatswain, and he starts ordering the kings to stay down below. William squared his shoulders and stuck out his chin and said, "'𝕴 pray now, keep below. 𝔜ou mar our labour: 𝕶eep your/cabins: 𝔜ou do assist the storm.'"

William began to recite by heart the argument between the old man named Gonzalo and the boatswain, where Gonzalo says, "'𝕴 have great comfort from this fellow: methinks he/hath no drowning mark upon him; his complexion is/ perfect gallows.'"

He stopped when he could tell by the blank looks of his audience that they weren't getting it. "What that meant," he told them, "is that Gonzalo is telling the bossy boatswain he looks like someone who was born to be hanged. You know what a gallows is, don't you? It's like this platform where they hang people." William pantomimed hanging, holding an imaginary rope above his tipped head and letting his tongue hang out. Gasps and giggles from his audience.

"And Gonzalo says he is feeling safer now, because if the boatswain was born to be hanged, he can't die by drowning. So that means the boat probably isn't going to sink after all." Jancy giggled, but the little kids still looked pretty vague.

William checked the book and told his audience, "The first scene ends with everybody still rocking back and forth in the storm, and then there's a big crashing sound like the boat just hit some rocks, and the curtain comes down real quick. And when it goes back up there are just two people onstage, sitting on a big rock on an island. One of them is an old man named Prospero and the other one is his beautiful daughter, Miranda. Miranda knows that her father can do magical things, so she's asking him if he caused the storm that sank the ship, because she feels sorry for the people who were in the boat. And then Prospero says to Miranda, '𝔅e collected:/ 𝔑o more amazement: tell your piteous heart/𝔗here's no harm done.' Which means that even though he did use magic to cause the storm, he hadn't let anybody drown. And that's when he tells Miranda to '𝔒pe thine ear' because he's going to explain everything to her."

It was right then that someone else said, "Oh, yes. I

remember that part now." And there was Clarice, sitting on the top step.

William was embarrassed. He had no idea how long she'd been sitting there and how much she'd seen and heard. He watched her face as she got up, but it was hard to tell what she was thinking. When she got down the stairs she stopped long enough to say hello to Ursa and the kids before she looked at William and said, "Why don't you do the part where you sing and dance?"

"Yes," Trixie and Buddy and even Jancy were saying. "Yes, sing and dance, William. Sing and dance."

He shook his head, grinning. "I didn't really dance," he told them. "Not like tap dancing or anything. I just twisted and twirled and jumped around and kind of halfway sang my lines. But I couldn't do it without a costume. You just can't do that kind of thing unless you're wearing a costume." He gestured at his dirty blue jeans and ragged T-shirt. "I can't do it like this. Later. Okay?"

Trixie sighed. "When, then?" she asked. "Tomorrow? Will you sing and dance tomorrow?"

"Well, not tomorrow," William said. "Tomorrow we'll be riding most of the day on the bus." And then, because Trixie looked so disappointed, he added, "On the bus to Gold Beach. Remember?"

That helped. "Yes," Trixie said. "Remember, Buddy?

Remember how nice it was there?" Buddy probably didn't, but he seemed to be willing to take Trixie's word for it. "Yeah," he said eagerly. "Gold Beach."

But then Clarice was pulling William aside and whispering in his ear. "Not tomorrow, I'm afraid," she said. "It would be very dangerous for you to go downtown tomorrow."

angerous? What do you mean?" William asked when Clarice said that it would be too dangerous for them to go to the downtown bus stop the next morning.

But she only put a finger to her lips and said, "I'll tell you later. Right now I need Jancy to help me make dinner for you guys. Come on, Jancy. We have to get your dinner over with, so the dishes and everything can be all cleaned up before my folks get home."

"I'll come too," William said, but Clarice said no, because someone had to babysit the kids in the basement until the food was ready, so they wouldn't run around the house and mess things up.

He tried to argue. To whisper urgently that you couldn't just tell a person that tomorrow would be dangerous, and then go off without explaining what you were talking about. But she wouldn't listen, and after she and Jancy went upstairs, he was left behind in the basement with Trixie and Buddy, listening to them whine about how much they wanted to go upstairs too.

"Come on, William. Let's go up to that big kitchen. We won't bother anything," Trixie said. "Tell Clarice we won't bother them while they're cooking dinner. Isn't that right, Buddy?"

"That's right," Buddy said. "We won't bother the kitchen. Tell Clice we just want to go up all those stairs again. Way up to that toy room."

That was what William was afraid of. Once they got in the house there was no telling where they'd wind up. "Nope," he told them. "Not yet. Soon, but not quite yet."

But they went on whining and begging until he finally offered to do the sailor on the sinking ship scene again if they'd shut up and be quiet. It worked, but it wasn't easy. William wound up reeling around being a sailor on a storm-tossed ship for so long that he was pretty seasick by the time Jancy finally came down to tell them dinner was ready.

The dinner was tuna and noodles. Not great, but better than most of the stuff Gertie managed to come up with. And there was more of it too, at least more than what was usually left when it finally got to be William's turn to fill his plate.

"Eat up," Clarice said. "There's plenty. I won't be eating much because I'll have to eat again when my parents get home."

"What will you and your parents have tonight?" Jancy asked. "What does your mom cook?"

"Nothing much," Clarice said. "Usually they eat at a restaurant near where they work and bring me home some of it. My mom's too busy to do much cooking. Before times got so bad, we used to have a live-in cook like my aunt does."

"Times got so bad?" William asked. "Even for lawyers?"

"Sure," Clarice said sarcastically. "Haven't you heard about the Depression? There's a big one right now. Even lawyers are depressed when the times are so bad people don't have enough money to sue each other."

William wasn't entirely sure he understood, but it was an interesting thing to think about. Or it would have been, if he still hadn't been so busy wondering what Clarice had meant when she said tomorrow would be dangerous. But he had to wait to find out until the food was gone. And then he had to wait some more while he and Jancy did the dishes and Clarice took the little kids up to pick out two more toys to borrow.

It wasn't until they were all back in the basement, with Trixie busy changing a baby doll's diaper and Buddy pushing a fancy toy car around in circles, that William finally managed to talk to Clarice alone. She was heading for the stairs when he grabbed her arm and whispered, "What did you mean about tomorrow being dangerous?

You'd better tell me, because we're leaving tomorrow morning no matter what. We have to."

Pulling away, Clarice stared at William haughtily. "Why do you have to? You can go on hiding here a little longer." She put her hands on her hips. "And you just better because . . ." She pulled William toward the stairs. "Because when I was downtown shopping, I noticed some things. Some important things."

"Like what?" William asked.

"Well, like . . ." Her eyes were jittery again, and when William looked at her, she looked away. But in a minute she went on. "Well, like . . . a lot of police cars."

"Police cars? Where?"

"All over town," she said. "Outside the grocery store, and . . ." She paused, and then nodded. "And down by the Greyhound bus station."

"Oh yeah?" A cold chill ran up the back of William's neck. "Around the bus station?" He stared at Clarice, and she stared back.

"Did it look like they were—well, looking for someone?"

Clarice nodded slowly. "Yeah," she said. "I think so. And that isn't all." She took a deep breath. "And—and there were posters, too. Yeah, there were posters pinned up on lampposts that said that four kids named Baggett were missing." She paused and then, "Oh yeah. The posters said there was a reward. That there'd be a reward for anybody who found them and told the police."

That sounded bad. Really bad. What it probably meant was that Big Ed must have made the posters, or had someone else make them. "What did it say on the posters? There weren't pictures, were there? Pictures of us on the posters?"

Clarice shook her head. "No," she said uncertainly. "No pictures. Just your names and how old you all are."

"Holy Toledo," William said. He was shocked, and his face must have shown it, because Clarice grabbed his arm and said, "What happened? Tell me about it."

"What do you mean? I don't know what the police are doing. Or who made the posters."

"No, I don't mean that," Clarice said. "I mean, what happened that made you decide to run away?" Her eyes were jumpy again, and her whole face looked stretched tight by excitement. "Did they kill somebody? Did the Baggetts finally kill somebody? I heard my dad say he thought they probably would, sooner or later."

William shook his head hard. "No," he said. "No. That wasn't it at all. They didn't kill anyone. It was just that—"

He didn't realize that Jancy had come up behind him until he heard her voice saying, "Yes, they did." She gave William a little shove. "Why don't you tell her? They killed Sweetie Pie. We ran away because they killed Sweetie Pie."

"Wow!" Clarice's voice had sunk to a loud whisper. "I knew it. I just knew there must have been a murder."

"Now, wait a minute," William said. "There wasn't any murder. Sweetie Pie was just a guinea pig."

It wasn't until he heard her gasp that William realized what he'd said, and he whirled around in time to see Jancy running across the room to throw herself facedown on her cot. Of course, he went after her.

It took a while. Sitting on the floor beside Jancy's cot, he patted her shoulder and told her he knew that Sweetie Pie was a lot more than *just* a guinea pig, and he shouldn't have put it that way. It wasn't until Jancy finally sat up and wiped the tears off her face and said she was okay, that he went back to where Clarice was waiting on the top stair.

He sat down beside her, and for a second or two they just looked at each other. Her eyes were still wide but not so fluttery looking, and after a minute she smiled—one of those strange, unexpected smiles. Nodding toward Jancy, she said, "That was good."

"What?" William said. "What was good?"

"What you did just then. What you said to Jancy." She paused and then went on, "Is Jancy her real name? It's not a normal-sounding name."

"I know," William said, grinning ruefully. "A lot of Baggetts have weird names. Big Ed named everybody. I think he'd decided to name the next one Johnny, but when she turned out to be a girl he just changed it to Jancy."

"Big Ed?" Clarice asked.

"Yeah. The Big Man. The Boss," William said sarcastically.

"You mean your father?"

William shrugged. "You might put it that way," he said.

Clarice nodded. "Well, anyway, it was nice what you said to Jancy. I heard you."

"Oh." William shrugged again. "Well, I shouldn't have said *just* a guinea pig. I mean, that guinea pig was the only pet Jancy ever had, and she was real crazy about it. And Sweetie Pie really *was* the reason we ran away when we did." He grinned. "I mean, it was Jancy who decided. Oh, I'd thought about doing it for a long time, but I didn't have any definite plans until Jancy decided it had to be right away."

Clarice nodded slowly. "Yes," she said. "I've thought a lot about running away too, and why a person might do it."

"You mean why we did it? I told you. It was what happened to Sweetie Pie that did it."

"That's not what I meant," she said. "What I meant was that I've thought about running away myself. About why I ought to do it."

William stared at Clarice, and she looked back. The

tense, nervous flicker was there in her eyes again, but it wasn't quite the same. William was puzzled.

"Why would you want to—," he was beginning to say, when she looked at her watch and jumped up.

"I'll tell you tomorrow," she said. "Okay? Tomorrow I'll tell you why I almost ran away, if you tell me first. I mean why you *really* decided to. Before the guinea pig thing."

William found himself agreeing. Tomorrow he would tell Clarice why he'd been planning to run away since he was about six years old. And she would tell him . . . what? He couldn't imagine.

She left then, and a few minutes later, as he was getting into his cot, Jancy sat up and motioned for him to come over, so he did. She wasn't crying anymore, but her eyelashes were still wet. "I won't be mad at you anymore," she said, "if you tell me what you and Clarice were talking about."

So he did. At least he told her the part about the police cars Clarice had seen in Crownfield, and how he'd decided they better not try to catch the bus tomorrow morning. But that was all. He didn't mention what Clarice had told him about running away. That could wait until he'd found out more about it himself.

The next day was Thursday, and just like the day before, they had to wait until Clarice's parents left for work before they went up to the kitchen for breakfast. The only difference was that while they were eating, Trixie kept asking why they weren't going to ride on the bus like William said. Of course that got Buddy started on the "why" thing too. From *why* weren't they going on the bus, he went on to *why* did they have to stay in the basement all day, and *why* did Clarice have so many toys, and *why* couldn't they pick out three toys to play with instead of just two, and *why* didn't everybody in the world have their own playroom with lots of toys? And a lot more.

At first Clarice seemed to think all the whys were amusing, but after a while she began to get glassy-eyed, and she interrupted Buddy's whys long enough to tell him that he could pick out three toys today, if he didn't say *why* one more time until he'd finished his breakfast. It worked. Both Buddy and Trixie ate silently and so fast they almost choked themselves, and it wasn't long before they were all back in the kitchen, loaded down with toys, and Clarice was telling Jancy it was her turn to babysit the kids in the basement while William helped do the dishes.

While he carried the dishes to the sink, William was feeling, along with some eager curiosity, a certain amount of uneasiness about having promised Clarice that he'd tell her why he'd been planning to run away. Things like how long he'd been planning to. For instance, the fact that as soon as he started school he'd begun to realize that most people lived in places that were cleaner, and quieter, and a lot more peaceful than any of the places he'd ever lived. And that most kids didn't get picked on and slapped around as much as he did. He'd never told anyone how he felt about being a Baggett, except, of course, Jancy. Not even Miss Scott, although he had a feeling that she knew about it without him having to tell her. Like how she seemed to know not to ask him if his parents were going to come to watch him being Ariel in 𝕿𝖍𝖊 𝕿𝖊𝖒𝖕𝖊𝖘𝖙.

Miss Scott. Now, that was a topic he'd rather talk about. Maybe he could start out by asking Clarice if she had Miss Scott for English last year, and go on from there. Go on to talk about how Miss Scott had picked him to be in 𝕿𝖍𝖊 𝕿𝖊𝖒𝖕𝖊𝖘𝖙, and taught him a whole lot, not only about 𝕾𝖍𝖆𝖐𝖊𝖘𝖕𝖊𝖆𝖗𝖊, but about stage presence and projection and a lot of other stuff about being an actor.

He knew it might not sidetrack Clarice. What she obviously wanted to hear was not just what happened to Jancy's Sweetie Pie, but also a lot of other stuff about the Baggetts. She'd probably love to hear things like how Big Ed never had a steady job because of his "bad back" and how his limp always got a lot worse whenever the welfare people came around. And how when he got drunk he yelled and hit everyone he could get his hands on, except the ones who were getting big enough to hit him back. And how the Baggetts had always moved around a lot because Big Ed hardly ever bothered to pay rent.

He was pretty sure those were the sorts of things Clarice wanted to hear. He didn't know how he knew, except the excited way her eyes started flickering whenever she started asking that kind of question. And he also knew that it was a subject he didn't particularly want to discuss.

But on the other hand, he had to admit that she wasn't the only one who was curious. He was curious about why in the world Clarice would be planning to run away. After all, she was the only child of very important people, like she kept saying, who apparently didn't slap her around, and certainly bought her everything she could possibly want, and then some.

Thinking ahead, it did occur to him that it might be possible to get Clarice to talk first, and maybe she'd get so wound up she'd keep going long enough so they would run out of time before they got to his turn. It seemed like a good idea, and it began to look even better when she took Jancy and the little kids down to the basement and didn't come back for a long time. Good. Not much time left before she'd have to leave to have lunch with her great-aunt.

"I know. I'm late," she said when she finally showed up. "Jancy asked for some soap and a scrub board so she could wash some clothes, so I had to show her how to use our new washing machine."

· "Washing machine?" William asked. "You have one of those machines that washes clothes?"

"Sure," Clarice said. "A new one with a big automatic wringer."

"An automatic wringer? Hey, I'd sure like to see that. All right?" William said, heading for the door. But it didn't work.

"You can see it later," Clarice said, starting the hot water running into the dishpan. "Right now we have some other things to do—and talk about. Okay. You first. Start talking." No argument or even discussion. Just "Start talking."

William sighed. There was the Miss Scott possibility, so he gave it a try. "Hey," he ventured. "Did you have Miss Scott for English last year?"

"Sure I did," Clarice said. "All the really good students do. Why?"

"I just wondered what you thought of her. You know, the way she taught English at the junior high and drama at the high school, too. I thought she was . . . Well, actually what a lot people think, is that she's . . . Well, a pretty good teacher."

Clarice shrugged. "Sure, she's okay, I guess. I've known her since I was just a little kid. I told you, she's a friend of my family." She paused and looked at William with squinty eyes. "Yeah, I guess you would think she's special. After all, she was the one who picked you to be Ariel." She did a slow grin. "How did that happen?" The grin faded. "Anyway, Miss Scott isn't what we were going to talk about. You were going to tell me how come you had to escape. I mean, what happened back there at the Baggetts' that made you decide you had to run away?"

Okay. He'd just see how much he could say without saying anything in particular. Picking up the dish towel, he dried several dishes before he said, "Well, my so-called father's name is Edward G. Baggett, and he's been married three times."

He paused to check Clarice. Disappointed, he thought. Nothing excitingly shocking about having three wives, as long as it's one at a time. So he went on. "His first wife had six kids, five boys and a girl, and his second wife, who was my mother, had four. Two of each. So that makes ten kids in one family."

"And what happened to his first wife?" Clarice interrupted. "Did she die?"

Actually, William didn't know. He remembered hearing Big Ed say that her name was Mabel and she came from Texas, but he'd never said where she went. So William told Clarice that he guessed Mabel just got tired of so many kids and went back to Texas. "And after that happened," he went on, "he married my mother, whose name was Laura Hardison, and she had me first and then Jancy, and a few years later, Trixie and Buddy. And a few days after she had Buddy, she died."

Clarice rinsed a plate, put it carefully in the rack, and turned to look at William with narrow eyes. "What did she die of?" she asked. "How old were you, and how did you feel about your mother dying like that?"

William returned her stare. Stared back, blank eyed and stiff faced. There was no way he was going to get into that. No way he would even begin to get into anything about his mother. Nothing about the way he'd felt about her when he was little and she took such good care of him and Jancy. But then, as he got older, how he began to blame her for letting Big Ed's older kids knock him around. And how sometimes, after Trixie was born, he'd almost hated his mother for spending all her time with the new baby, and kind of giving up on him and Jancy.

Maybe he'd just say something that would give Clarice the thrill she was obviously looking for. Something that wouldn't be too far from the truth, either. Like, for instance, "She died of being a Baggett." But no, he wouldn't. Instead he just said, "I don't remember. But when she died, her sister, Fiona Hardison, came and took Buddy and Trixie to live with her for two years. Then Ed Baggett got married again, so he just went to her house and took them back."

"So now you have a stepmother?" Clarice's eyes narrowed again, probably thinking *evil stepmother* like in a fairy tale.

"Yeah, I guess so," William said.

"What do you mean, you guess so? If she's married to your father, she's your stepmother. Right?"

"Right." William shrugged. "I guess." He didn't go on to say that it had never occurred to him to think of Gertie Baggett as his mother, step or otherwise.

"So when did you start thinking about running away?" Clarice's eyes still had that sharp, squinty look. "And why? What happened that made you decide that's what you had to do?"

William looked at the clock on the kitchen wall. "Look what time it is," he said. "You're going to have to leave for your aunt's house pretty soon. So it's your turn to talk now. Okay?"

She frowned at first and shook her head, but at last she said, "Well, okay. *Okay*." It took a while before she began again. "Like I told you, my parents are very important people." There it was again, that sharp, sarcastic edge to the positive, almost boastful, things she was saying. "They're both lawyers, you know, and my father might be a judge pretty soon if the times start getting better. They met each other way back when they were in law school, and they decided to open an office together and get married." Long pause. "But I don't think they ever decided to have any children."

She looked at William, so he looked back, but he didn't say anything until after she repeated, slowly and significantly, "I don't think they ever decided to have children."

At last William grinned and said, "Well, I guess that's the way it happens sometimes. I guess people can have kids without actually deciding to."

She didn't smile. "So what they *did* decide to do was to pretend it didn't happen, at least as much as they possibly could. Like when I was little they hired a live-in babysitter to keep me from bothering them too much, and now they have me spend most of my time at my great-aunt's house. Or at least they think that's what I'm doing. And then they go and buy me all sorts of stupid junk just so everybody will think that they're these great, wonderful, devoted parents."

"And so?" William nodded, thinking, *Is that it?* But what he said out loud was just, "And so *that's* the reason you decided to run away?"

He didn't say anything more. Not a word about what was really going through his mind, but she must have kind of guessed.

"All right," she said. "All right! So they didn't beat me or shut me up in a dungeon or anything. But how would you feel if you knew your parents thought you were just a big mistake? How would you feel if . . ." She kind of ran down then and went on staring at William for a minute before she shrugged and said, "Well, I never did get around to making any actual plans to run away, I guess. But I do think about it sometimes. You know. Like, sometimes I wonder if they'd even notice I was gone."

She turned away then and went back to washing the dishes very hard and fast. She didn't say anything more until the dishpan had been put away. Then she grabbed a plate out of William's hands and said, "No. The plates don't go there. They go up here. *See?*"

"Yeah," he said. "I see." And he did. Where the plates went, and a few other things besides.

Life in the Ogdens' basement went pretty smoothly that morning, at least for a while. There were a lot of toys to keep the little kids busy. Jancy had borrowed a couple of books from Clarice's bookshelves, and after she'd finished hanging the still ragged, but much cleaner, clothes up to dry, she got to read for a while too.

And William himself even managed to spend an hour or so reading **Twelfth Night**—the part where Sir Andrew Aguecheek, one of Sir Toby's drinking buddies, comes onstage and tries to get friendly with Maria, the chambermaid, except she lets him know she definitely isn't interested.

William found he was able to read most of a page without having to look up more than a couple of words in the glossary at the back of the book, and he probably would have gotten even further if he hadn't had some other things on his mind. Things like how he was going to get everybody to Aunt Fiona's now that the police were looking for them. Reading **Shakespeare**, he decided, is a lot harder when the police are looking for you.

It wasn't until after lunch—sandwiches in the basement again—that the kids got tired of playing with their toys and began begging William to let them go outside.

"No, you know Clarice said you can't do that," he told them.

"I know that," Trixie said. "But I don't know—"

"*Why*," Buddy finished her sentence. "*Why* can't we play outside, Willum?"

Thinking that *because the police might see you* would sound too scary, William could only say, "Because the neighbors might see you."

Trixie thought about that for a minute before she asked, "Why don't we want the neighbors to see us? We won't do anything bad."

"Yeah," Buddy echoed. "We won't do anything bad."

William considered *because the neighbors might tell Big Ed* but decided that might be even scarier, so he could only shrug and try to get back into 𝕾𝖍𝖆𝖐𝖊𝖘𝖕𝖊𝖆𝖗𝖊. But the whys kept coming, one after another until he suddenly blew his top and bellowed, "Stop it! No more whys." It wasn't until both the little kids, and even Jancy, stared at him, wide-eyed, that he realized how much he'd sounded like a Baggett.

"Okay, okay," he told them. "If you forget about going outside, I'll do some more of 𝕿𝖍𝖊 𝕿𝖊𝖒𝖕𝖊𝖘𝖙. Would you like that?"

They would, but he'd barely opened his 𝕯𝖔𝖚𝖇𝖑𝖊𝖉𝖆𝖞'𝖘 𝕮𝖔𝖒𝖕𝖑𝖊𝖙𝖊 𝖂𝖔𝖗𝖐𝖘 𝖔𝖋 𝖂𝖎𝖑𝖑𝖎𝖆𝖒 𝕾𝖍𝖆𝖐𝖊𝖘𝖕𝖊𝖆𝖗𝖊 to page 1300 when the basement door opened and Clarice came in and sat down on the steps.

"Hey," she said. "You going to do some more Shakespeare? Go on, do it. I'll watch too."

William swallowed hard. Having Clarice in the audience made a difference. Maybe he'd just forget about it. Cancel the performance. But then he looked back to where Jancy, two bug-eyed little kids, and one very attentive, very large dog, were sitting up straight in a neat row. Sighing, he reached out again for his 𝕮𝖔𝖒𝖕𝖑𝖊𝖙𝖊 𝖂𝖔𝖗𝖐𝖘 and turned it so the kids could all see the picture on the cover. The picture of Prospero and Miranda on their little island, surrounded by a stormy sea.

"See, here they are. Prospero and Miranda. Right here on the cover."

Trixie and Buddy, and Jancy, too, crowded closer. "Is that Miranda?" Jancy asked. "How old is she?"

"She must be fifteen," William said. "Because she was three when they came to the island, and they've been there for twelve years. So she must be fifteen."

"Oh, fifteen," Trixie said. "Just like Babe."

William shrugged and grinned. "Well, not exactly like Babe."

"No," Trixie said. "She's a lot more beautiful than Babe, that's for sure. Is she more beautiful than I am?

Who's most beautiful, Buddy? Me or Miranda?"

Buddy pushed Trixie out of the way and stared at the drawing. Tilting his head one way and then the other, he looked from Trixie to the picture and back again before he pointed at the picture and said, "She is."

Trixie glared at Buddy, and he glared back. They were still glaring when Jancy told them to sit down and be quiet. "Sit down and watch William," she said. "He's going to tell what happened next after the storm. Remember, where Miranda's father told her to ope her ear and he'd tell her about the tempest."

Pulling the sheet off his cot, William wrapped it around his shoulders like a cape and sat down. Holding out a hand the way Prospero was doing in the picture, he recited from memory, "'Canst thou remember/A time before we came unto this cell?/J do not think thou canst, for then thou wast not/out three years old.'"

Then he jumped up. Wrapping the sheet around his waist like a long skirt, and talking in a higher voice, he said, "''Tis far off/And rather like a dream . . . /Had J not/Four or five women once that tended me?'"

Readjusting the sheet again, William said, "'Thou hadst, and more, Miranda. . . . Twelve year since, Miranda, twelve year since,/Thy father was the Duke of Milan and/A prince of power.'"

Trixie's hand was waving in the air, and when William looked at her, she said, "But I thought Prospero was her father."

William grinned. "You're right," he said. "Just listen. Miranda's very next line is . . ." Rearranging the sheet and raising his voice, he said, "'Sir, are not you my father?'"

Deciding that the next part was going to need a little more explaining, William said, "So then Prospero starts telling Miranda about how he'd always liked to do all kinds of magic. And then he got so busy reading and studying about magic, he let his brother, whose name was Antonio, kind of run the kingdom for him."

"I remember," Jancy interrupted. "You said to remember Antonio because he was the bad guy."

"Right," William said. "He was so bad that he decided he wanted to take Prospero's place and be the Duke of Milan, so he had his servants kidnap Prospero and Miranda, who was only three years old, and put them in a little boat way out on the ocean all by themselves. And they probably would have died, except the good old man named Gonzalo had put a lot of food and water in the boat. And he put all of Prospero's books about how to do magic in the boat too. So then Miranda says, 'And now, I pray you, sir,/For still 'tis beating in my mind, your reason/For raising this sea-storm?'"

After checking Prospero's next speech, William decided it would be quicker and easier to explain it in his own words, so he could get on quickly to the first place where it says, Enter Ariel.

"So then Prospero tells her," he said, "that it just

happened that his worst enemies, like his brother Antonio and Alonzo, the king of Naples, were on the ship, and that's why he raised the storm that made the ship sink. But remember, he also told Miranda that he didn't let anybody get hurt."

William threw off the sheet and said, "And now comes the good part. Now I'm going to be Ariel."

But right at that moment Clarice jumped up from where she'd been sitting on the stairs and yelled, "Wait a minute. Wait till I get back," and ran up the stairs and out the door.

They waited quite a while. Finally Trixie said angrily, "Where did she go? Why did she run off like that, just when you were getting to the good part?"

"Who knows?" Jancy said.

"Maybe she had to go to the baffroom," Buddy said.

"No," Trixie said. "I don't think so. If she had to go to the bathroom, she could have gone in the one down here."

But Buddy stuck to his baffroom theory, and they were still arguing about it when the door banged open and Clarice came down the stairs carrying some strange-looking pieces of cloth, things that looked like long stockings and a bunch of filmy see-through stuff.

"Here." She pushed the bundle into William's arms. "Put these on. And when you come out, I'll be Prospero."

"How are you going to—," William had started to say when she interrupted.

"From the book," she said. "Just show me where."

So William pointed out Prospero's next speech before he went in to dress, and while he was gone Clarice studied her lines for a minute and then reached into her pocket and got out some matches and a couple of Fourth of July sparklers.

Wrapping herself in the bedsheet cloak, she told the little kids, "See, William is going to be this super-magical spirit named Ariel, who was trapped in a tree trunk until Prospero rescued him. So he has to obey everything Prospero says. And just now he's coming back from setting the ship on fire in the middle of the storm, and he's going to say that he's done everything Prospero wanted him to. I'll be Prospero, but wait till you see how William does the part about setting everything on fire. In the play at Crownfield High, he had this long, thin flashlight that looked like a torch, but these sparklers will look almost as good." She got up and stood by the bathroom and shouted, "Tell me when you're ready and I'll light a sparkler. Okay?"

Up until that moment William had been reluctant, but suddenly he began to feel the way he had when he was on the stage at the high school and people were cheering and clapping. Pulling on the black tights and loose filmy tunic that Clarice had provided, he became the magical sprite Ariel.

Stopping only long enough to snatch a lighted sparkler from Clarice's hand, William bounded, leaped, and twirled dramatically before coming back to make a sweeping bow before Clarice, who, with one finger on the top of page 1302, recited, "'𝔍 am ready now./ Approach, my 𝔄riel, come.'"

"'𝔄ll hail, great master! 𝔊rave sir, hail,'" William/Ariel cried. "'𝔍 come/𝔗o answer thy best pleasure; be't to fly,/𝔗o swim, to dive into the fire, to ride/𝔒n the curl'd clouds, to thy strong bidding task/𝔄riel and all his quality.'"

Moving her finger down the page, Clarice said, "'𝔥ast thou, spirit,/𝔓erform'd to point the tempest that 𝔍 bade thee?'"

That was when William got to do his best scene. Leaping and whirling around the stage, he waved his torch, pretending to be setting everything on the ship on fire, and shouted, "'𝔑ow in the waist, the deck, in every cabin,/𝔍 flamed amazement: sometime 𝔍'd divide,/𝔄nd burn in many places; on the topmast,/𝔗he yards and bowsprit, would 𝔍 flame distinctly,/𝔗hen meet and join.'"

That had been where the whole auditorium full of people usually cheered and clapped. But now, pausing long enough to check out his audience, William decided that their silence didn't mean they hadn't appreciated his performance. Jancy had her hands clasped under her chin, and her smile was wide and quivery. Both of the little kids were round-eyed and openmouthed, and even Ursa was up on his feet, panting excitedly.

The expression on Clarice's face was different. Different and uncomfortably concentrated. William looked away quickly.

And then Buddy was saying, "Do it again, Willum."

And Trixie said, "Oh yes. Please do it again. Please, please."

He was actually thinking he might when Clarice suddenly looked at her watch and gasped. "Oh no. I have to go," she said, and started up the stairs.

"What is it?" Jancy called after her. "Is somebody coming?"

"No," Clarice called back. "But something might be burning." At the door she stopped only long enough to throw Prospero's robe down the stairs before she disappeared.

"Burning?" Trixie was worried. "What's burning? Is the house on fire? Maybe you did it with those sparkler things, William."

They looked around anxiously, checking out all the places William had touched with his sparkler torch. Nothing seemed to be on fire, but they were all feeling a little uneasy, right up until Clarice came back down the stairs and told them that dinner was ready. And when Buddy asked, "What burned up, Clice?" she shrugged and said it was only the chicken.

Chicken! Forgetting all about Ariel and his fire-setting dance, they all headed for the kitchen where, right there in a big roasting pan, was a whole chicken, surrounded by potatoes and carrots, all roasted and ready to eat. The chicken was just a little black along one edge, but it still looked and smelled very good.

When there had been chicken at the Baggetts, none of the smaller kids, and that included William, ever got anything better than a neck or a few scraps of skin. And now there were just the four of them for a really big chicken. Clarice, again, wasn't eating much because she would eat later with her parents. So there were drumsticks or thighs for everybody. And when William said how good it was, Clarice just went on apologizing for letting it burn.

"It's not really burned," William told her. "But what I don't get is how you cooked a great meal like this all by yourself." He paused and raised an eyebrow before he went on, "And how are you going to keep your folks from finding out about it?"

Clarice shrugged. "Easy," she said. "Edith, my great-aunt's maid, is teaching me how to cook, and roast chicken is one of her specialties, because that's Aunt Pearl's favorite meal. And don't worry about where the chicken and all that stuff came from. I just went on downtown while I was on my way to my aunt's house and got what I needed. And Mr. Griffith, he's the grocer, just thought I was shopping for my aunt."

"But what if he says something about it to your aunt? Like how was the chicken, or like that?" Jancy asked.

Clarice shook her head. "He won't ask her," she said. "Aunt Pearl doesn't talk to anybody much. Particularly not people in grocery stores."

But William was still worried. "But what about all the money it cost?" He motioned to all the food in the big roasting pan. "That must have cost a whole lot."

She shrugged again and insisted, "Don't worry about it. Okay?"

But William did worry about it. He even thought of offering to pay her some of what she must have spent. He knew that his running-away fund had thirty-one dollars and seventeen cents in it, which seemed like a lot. Probably more than enough to buy the tickets to Gold Beach. And there was no good reason why someone who hardly knew them should be buying expensive food for a bunch of runaway kids.

"Look," he started to tell Clarice, "I have some money. Maybe I could pay for some—"

"I *said*, don't worry about it," Clarice told him. Leaning over with her lips close to William's ear, she whispered something he didn't quite hear. It started out, "You know, like I told you . . ." before it turned into a bunch of sizzling sounds.

He didn't want her to do it again, so he said, "All right. All right. But thanks anyhow. It sure was good."

When everyone had eaten as much as they possibly could, William told Jancy to take the little kids and Ursa back to the basement, and he'd be there as soon as he helped with the dishes. It was really Jancy's turn to do dishes, but there were things that William needed to discuss with Clarice.

As soon as they were alone, he started asking the kind of questions he really needed answers to, like what she had seen this time, when she was downtown. Questions like, "When you were there, did you see a lot of police cars again, or posters about missing kids?"

"Police cars?" Clarice said. "No, I didn't. . . ." She paused for a minute and then said, "Oh, yes. *Those* police cars." She nodded. "I did see two, or maybe it was three. And another poster. Yes. I did see another really big poster." She held out her arms to show how big it had been.

William couldn't help wincing. "I was afraid of that. Were the posters near the bus station?"

"Oh yes, near the bus station. There was a police car right there near the bus station too."

"But you didn't . . ." He hardly dared ask. "You didn't see any of the Baggetts, did you?"

"Baggetts?" Clarice looked doubtful. Shaking her head, she said, "I'm not sure if I'd know whether someone was a Baggett or not."

"Yeah." William nodded ruefully. "You'd know, I think." He hunched his shoulders, and letting his arms swing wide with clenched fists, he stuck out his chin and stomped around the kitchen, glaring first in one direction and then in another. "Like this," he said. "Only bigger. A *lot* bigger."

Clarice giggled like crazy while William pretended not to notice as he went on glaring from side to side. A good actor doesn't laugh at his own funny business. But then Clarice finally sobered up enough to say, "Yes, I did." She nodded firmly. "Yes, I think I did see a couple of guys who looked just like that."

But suddenly William didn't believe her. Not about seeing Baggetts, and not really about the police cars and posters, either. Something, he didn't know what, was making him feel pretty sure that she wasn't telling the truth.

Later that night when the little kids were asleep,

one at each end of their cot, William pushed his cot a little nearer to Jancy's and started telling her about what Clarice had said, and what his reaction had been.

"She said," he told Jancy, "that there were still police cars downtown near the bus station. And that she saw some people who looked like they might be Baggetts. Only the thing was . . ." He paused, checking back to remember how certain he'd suddenly been. "The thing was, I'm pretty sure she was lying." He shook his head. "I don't know why, but I just got this feeling that she was telling a bunch of lies. I don't know why she would do something like that, but I think she did."

At first Jancy looked surprised and shocked. "Why do you suppose she'd do that?" she asked. "Why would she lie to you about there being police cars and Baggetts in Crownfield?"

He shrugged. "I don't know. Unless it's just that she doesn't want us to leave, at least not right away. I think that might be it. Yesterday she told me some stuff that made me think she's sort of lonely. So maybe she likes having some extra people around." He grinned. "Even if they're just a bunch of Baggetts."

Jancy didn't smile. She seemed to be thinking for quite a while before she nodded slowly and thoughtfully. "Maybe," she said. "But I don't think that's the reason. Not exactly, at least."

"Oh yeah? What is it then?"

"I think it's mostly *you* she doesn't want to go away. That's what I think."

William was puzzled. "Why do you think that?"

Jancy ducked her head and looked at William out of the tops of her eyes. She was smiling, but there was something about her tone of voice that made it sound like an accusation. "You're the one she's crazy about," she said.

William was shocked and indignant. "What? What are you talking about?"

Jancy shrugged. "Well, that's just what I think." Her eyes suddenly opened wider. "Either that, or else it's Ariel. Yeah. Maybe it's Ariel she's in love with."

William might have argued some more, but just then Trixie woke up and kicked Buddy, and Buddy woke up enough to kick her back and start mumbling. Which meant he'd better be taken to the bathroom right away.

So William got Buddy up and walked him to the bathroom, and by the time they were both back in bed, Jancy was either asleep, or pretending to be.

William didn't sleep very well that night. All night long he kept waking up to lie there wide-eyed, going over his plans. Plans that now seemed to include not only how to escape the Baggetts, but also . . . He couldn't help grinning a little. How to escape Clarice?

It was an interesting, if sort of embarrassing, complication. Not that he thought for a moment that Jancy knew what she was talking about when she said that Clarice was in love with him. That, of course, was a joke. Enough to make any halfway sensible person laugh. He chuckled to himself.

But then there was that other idea that Jancy had come up with. The one about it being Ariel that Clarice was in love with. Now that, he decided, might be a little more likely. After all, wasn't it true that lots of people were sort of in love with actors or actresses whom they'd seen only as characters in the movies, or on the stage? And hadn't Clarice first seen him, really noticed him at least, when he was being Ariel on the high school auditorium's stage? It was something to think about.

But that meant—he sighed deeply—he not only had to somehow get himself and Jancy and the little kids away from the house and down to the bus stop without being seen by the police or the Baggetts, but also without having their getaway sabotaged by Clarice. And what's more, it was going to have to happen very soon, since tomorrow would be Friday. Clarice hadn't mentioned it, but her parents were probably home all day on weekends—which would make hiding a bunch of Baggetts in the basement a lot trickier. If not impossible.

There was, it seemed, only one thing to do. One dangerous but maybe not impossible thing. Before he went back to sleep, he had it all planned. What he was going to have to do was go, all by himself, on a scouting trip to find out not only what time a Greyhound bus would be heading toward Gold Beach on Saturday morning, and how much the tickets cost, but also whether or not Clarice had been lying about the town being full of posters and police cars. He lay there for a long time planning his trip. Having lived in at least a half dozen places all over Crownfield before the Baggetts got kicked out of town, he knew the whole downtown area pretty well, so it shouldn't be too hard to decide which route would be safest, and where he might find some hiding places if he needed them. When he finally did go to sleep, he had this awful dream about being chased all over town by a whole lot of angry Baggetts who kept jumping out at him from behind corners, and even crawling out from under parked cars, looking like alligators wearing boots and black leather jackets.

But morning finally came, and he and Jancy got up and kept the little kids quiet until they heard the car leaving. Then Clarice came down to get them and breakfast was pancakes again, and everything was pretty much the same as before. Except that William couldn't help being on the lookout for any signs that Jancy was right about Clarice.

He couldn't really believe it. Especially after he sized himself up in the mirror over the sideboard. Carefully checked out his bony face and scrawny body, and then did the same with Clarice. She really wasn't all that bad looking, he decided, particularly now and then when she happened to be smiling.

Not a chance, he told himself. *Jancy has a big imagination.* But then there *was* the Ariel possibility. That was, perhaps, something else again. Testing it out, he tried to get into an Ariel frame of mind. Not that he started leaping and twirling, but he did try to bring to mind the wild, free, unlimited feeling he'd always gotten when he was onstage. And it sort of worked. Right about then, when he caught Clarice looking at him, he thought he saw a hint of what Jancy had been talking about, in the way her eyelids were kind of fluttering.

But so what? All that meant was he was going to have to be particularly careful today not to let Clarice know what he was planning. Not to say a thing about what he would be doing the minute she left to go shopping and make her midday visit to her aunt's.

And he didn't. Not a word while the kitchen was cleaned up, the kids were escorted up to get a new batch of toys, and a bunch of leftovers from last night's feast were packed up to be carried down to the basement for lunch. But then Clarice got on her bicycle and rode off, and it was time to start.

Actually it wasn't until then, when Clarice was gone and the little kids were busy playing, that he told Jancy what he was getting ready to do, and at first she hated the idea a whole lot.

"But I have to," William kept telling her. "We can't drag the little kids through town and down to the bus station without knowing whether or not Clarice was telling the truth about the police and everything. And without even knowing for sure what time the bus leaves for Gold Beach."

When he got that far, Jancy was still shaking her head, but then he went on, "Or even if I really have enough money for four tickets."

That did it. Jancy's big eyes got even bigger, and she bit her lower lip for a while before she said, "Okay. Okay. I guess you have to. But just be awful careful, William."

Grabbing him by both arms, she shook him and repeated, "Please, please, be awful careful."

"Don't worry," he told her. "I sure will." And he couldn't have meant it more. He certainly wasn't looking forward to going as far as the Greyhound bus station through a town where anyone might know about the mysterious disappearance of the four youngest Baggetts and be all prepared to throw him in jail and call Big Ed. The very thought was enough to give him that heart-racing, throat-shrinking feeling.

"I wish there was some way we could sort of disguise you," Jancy was saying.

"Like what?" he asked.

She thought for a moment, then said, "Hey. Wait a minute." She took off, running up out of the basement and then, as William lagged behind, on up to disappear into the kitchen. It wasn't long before she returned, carrying a bunch of clothing over her arm.

"What's that?" William wanted to know. "What's that stuff?"

"Come up here," Jancy said, so he did, and when he got into the kitchen she went on, "It's some real nice boys' clothing I saw in that hall coat closet yesterday. You know, when Buddy ran off and I was looking all over for him. I asked Clarice whose they were, and she said they belonged to her cousin who came to visit last Easter, and when he went off he left this suit, because he'd pretty much outgrown it. It looks like it might fit you."

William checked the things out. There were some pants made of a smooth gray material with built-in pleats down the front, a dressy grayish brown checked jacket, and a floppy cap made of the same material as the jacket.

"I can't wear that," William said. But of course he did. The pants were a little too big around his waist and the jacket sleeves were just a bit long. But it was the matching cap that was the most important. Pulling the silk-lined cap down hard over his shaggy hair made him look a whole lot different. And feel different too. Almost as if he were wearing a stage costume. A kind of rich-kid costume that you'd certainly never see on anybody in a play about runaway Baggetts, that was for sure. But an excellent costume for someone who was playing the role of a self-confident guy who knew what he wanted, and how to go about getting it.

It was in that frame of mind that he waved good-bye to a stunned-looking Jancy and started down Gardenia, even managing to stay in character when he met up with a Gardenia Street resident. An oldish guy with a cane and a lot of white hair, who smiled and nodded in such an enthusiastic way that it was obvious that he had no idea he'd just met up with a Baggett.

That meeting put William into a confident mood that he managed to hang on to all the way down Gardenia

Street, and almost to Main. But on Main Street, in a part
of the city that he'd known very well when the Baggetts
were living in town, he found it harder to keep on feeling
and acting like a visiting tourist who actually lived in
some famous place like London or Paris.

Out on Main Street the first thing he did was stop
long enough to check up and down the street for police
cars. Not even one. And no posters, either, at least not
on any of the lampposts he'd passed so far. So much for
Clarice's horror stories.

But now, right there in front of him was Carson's
Candy Store, where, when he was four or five years old,
Al and Andy used to twist his arm until he agreed to
go in and look pitiful until the kind lady behind the
counter gave him a handful of jelly beans. Which he, of
course, had to turn over to the twins the minute he got
outside—or get slapped around. And get slapped around
even harder if he'd dared to eat even one of them.

And down there on the corner was Wally's Cheap
Gas, where the older Baggett brothers always used to
go to buy gasoline for their hot rods and motorcycles.
William was still staring at the familiar shapes of the
gas tanks when an even more familiar screeching roar
made him head for cover. A motorcycle was thundering
into Wally's driveway. A motorcycle with two big shaggy
windblown guys on the seat. Without waiting to be sure,
Baggetts or not, William jumped around the corner into

the alley and stayed there, completely out of sight for several minutes, until the motor roared again—roared and then died away.

Close call. Way too close. Ducking his camouflaged head in its floppy cap, William walked hard and fast in the direction of the Greyhound bus station. The next scary question was, would the clerk on duty today be someone he'd met before? Someone who'd known him well enough to see through his rich kid costume and immediately call the police? As he pushed open the door to the ticket office, William held his breath.

Well, hello there, young man," the man under the picture of a huge dog with a skinny middle, said. Not a familiar face. Whew! Big relief.

Taking a deep breath, William started to talk in the relaxed, self-confident way that a person would expect from a kid whose cap matched his jacket. "Hello there, sir. My name is Wilbur—er, Jones, yeah, Jones—and my parents sent me down to inquire about your schedule for Saturday morning. Like, when the first bus for Gold Beach leaves. And oh yes"—his slight shrug was supposed to indicate that whatever the answer might be, it wasn't likely to cause any big problem—"they would like to know the price of a ticket to Gold Beach."

"Would they now?" The man lifted one eyebrow. A look that might mean he was suspicious—or maybe just amused. "Well, I'm afraid I've a bit of bad news for your parents."

William stiffened with apprehension.

"I'm afraid our northern route doesn't actually go through Gold Beach," the clerk went on. "But the bus that leaves here at seven fifteen does make a stop in Reedly. Do you suppose that would do? Gold Beach and Reedly are only three or four miles apart."

William gulped and managed to say, "Three or four miles . . ." Getting a grip on himself and concentrating on his rich city kid role, he said, "Oh, sure. Close enough, I guess. We can always catch a cab from there, I suppose. Thanks a lot." He turned to go and then, remembering the other important question that really needed an answer, turned back. "And the price?" he asked. "How much is a ticket to Reedly?"

"Well now, let's just look that up. Just to be sure." The clerk was obviously talking down to him as if he were some little kid. But William was in no mood to try to set him straight. After the guy ran his finger down a couple of lists he said, "Two dollars and fifty cents." His grin widened. "That's for adults, however. Only two dollars for anyone in the family who just might not be twelve years old."

Great. He had plenty of money. William was so relieved he wasn't even tempted to inform the smart-aleck clerk that the person he was talking to would, in fact, be turning thirteen in only a month.

Outside the Greyhound station he pulled his cap down over his eyes and walked fast until he was past

Wally's Gas and the candy store. Cars went by. Mostly nice, clean, newish vehicles that weren't likely to be carrying Baggetts. But then a beat-up pickup that looked suspiciously . . . But no, the white-haired driver wasn't anyone that William knew. Another big *whew!*

There were pedestrians, too, and two or three of them looked vaguely familiar, like people he might have seen before, and who might recognize him as one of the missing Baggetts. But each time, the dangerous not-complete-stranger went right on by. It was the cap that saved him, he was sure of that, along with his ability to play a role. In this case, the role of a rich-kid relative of the Ogden family.

Two or three more pedestrians went by without gasping or staring, before William reached the comparative safety of Gardenia Street. Once there, walking faster and faster, he quickly arrived at the driveway that led down to the large, brown-shingled home of the well-known Ogden family. A home whose solid, respectable appearance certainly wouldn't cause anyone to suspect that a bunch of Baggetts were holed up in the basement.

But not any longer, William told himself as he started down the steps that led to the basement. *Tomorrow we're out of here.*

When he reached out for the latch, the basement door flew open and there was Jancy, looking as wild-eyed as if she'd just seen an ogre, or perhaps her fairy godmother.

"Oh, William," she kind of gasped. "You're all right. You are all right, aren't you? Did you see anyone who knew who you were?"

"Not a soul," William said. "And not even one policeman. Just like I told you, Clarice must have been making stuff up about all the police cars and everything, just to keep us from leaving."

Jancy managed a shaky grin. "Just to keep *you* from leaving, anyway," she said. He ignored her.

Rather reluctantly William got out of his rich-kid costume, and the rest of that day passed pretty much the same as before, except that William and Jancy managed to sneak in a few minutes of secret planning now and then. Secret because, if they knew what was about to happen, there was no way in the world Trixie and Buddy would be able to keep their mouths shut when Clarice showed up that afternoon. Not even if they'd been warned that they mustn't tell her. Which meant that all the real packing would have to be done after the little kids were asleep that evening.

"And then we'll have to get them up in time to leave for the bus station by a little after six," William said.

"Will that be early enough?" Jancy asked.

William nodded uncertainly. "I think so. It's only about ten blocks to downtown, but with all the stuff we'll be lugging, including Buddy if we can't wake him up, we better have almost an hour."

"About all our clothes and stuff—," Jancy was beginning when William interrupted.

"I know. That's a problem. I don't think we should drag that flour sack and pillow case downtown with us. I mean, if we do, people are bound to get suspicious. I'm afraid we'll just have to shove as much clothing as we can into my knapsack and leave the rest behind."

Jancy sighed and shook her head. "But your knapsack is pretty full already with just your stuff in it. And if we leave most of our clothes here, what about when Aunt Fiona finds out that she has to go right out and buy us all something to wear? She just might—she might decide not to . . ."

Jancy stammered to a stop, but she'd already said enough to make William realize that he wasn't the only one who was worried about what Fiona Hardison would do when four hungry, shabby, uninvited kids showed up on her doorstep. But a minute later when Jancy pleaded, "Couldn't you leave that big, heavy **Shakespeare** book here? Just for now, so we can take all our clothes? If you write Clarice a letter once we get to Gold Beach, maybe she'll mail it to you." Jancy's grin was slightly teasing as she went on, "I'll bet you a hundred dollars she would if you wrote her a real nice letter and signed it, 'Love, William.'"

William gave her a cold stare. "Where I go, **Shakespeare** goes," he told her so firmly she didn't bother to ask again.

Jancy made that suggestion about leaving Shakespeare behind in the early afternoon, while the little kids were busy playing tug-of-war with Ursa. It was nearly two o'clock and almost time for Clarice to come back from her aunt's house when Jancy came up with another crazy idea. She'd been prowling around the basement looking in some of the cabinets, and now she came over and tugged at William's arm.

"Look what I found," she said, and pulled him toward a large cabinet in the back of the big room. Opening the tall double doors, she said, "See, suitcases. All kinds of suitcases."

William gave her an even colder stare. "You don't mean we——," he began, but she interrupted.

"It wouldn't be stealing. We could leave a note telling the Ogdens that we borrowed one of their suitcases, and when we get to Aunt Fiona's we'll send it back to them. And look, maybe we could take just that old-looking one way down there at the bottom. They probably don't use that one anymore, anyway. "

At first William was against the whole idea, and he told Jancy so. Told her how one of the first Shakespeare quotes Miss Scott had taught her class was, "Neither a borrower nor a lender be." But when he'd had time to think about it, he realized that what Jancy was saying really did make sense. If they left a note, it wouldn't actually be stealing. And it *would* be a lot safer to appear in the bus station looking like part of a normal tourist-type family, instead of a bunch of tramps. Or runaways?

But there was another possibility. "Wait a minute," William said. "Maybe it would be all right to just go ahead and tell Clarice that we have to leave. You know, because tomorrow will be Saturday. She must know that there's no way we could stay here on a weekend with her folks home all day." He grinned. "We could mention how lawyer-type people like her parents aren't likely to take kindly to having a bunch of people the police are looking for right here in their own house. If we put it to her that way—make her see what might happen—I bet she'd say, 'Okay, go. Get out.'"

He acted that last part out, stamping his foot and pointing dramatically as he said, "Okay, go! Get out!" But before he even finished the act, Jancy started shaking her curly head, and went on shaking it for a long time after he finished his dramatic scene.

At last she said, "William. You are *so* wrong. If we tell Clarice we're going to leave, she'll find some way to stop us. Believe me."

He didn't. Not really. But then again, maybe he just didn't understand women. So maybe he'd better listen to what Jancy was saying. He sighed. "Yeah, well, I guess you might be right. Looks like we better not tell her."

It was only a few minutes after they'd finally settled the suitcase argument, when Clarice showed up carrying a big grocery bag. She said hi to everyone and told the kids that dinner was almost ready. But then she motioned for William and Jancy to come sit on the steps with her. "We have to talk," she said. And as soon as they were seated she began. "It's about weekends."

Weekends, William noticed. Not this weekend, but *weekends*. As if she were planning on a lot of them. Jancy got it too. She caught William's eye and lifted an eyebrow before she ducked her head and hid her face.

"Yeah. We were wondering about the weekend," William said. "Aren't your folks home all day on Saturdays and Sundays?"

"Well, sometimes," Clarice said. "Except tomorrow they're both going to a Chamber of Commerce lunch that starts around eleven and always lasts most of the afternoon, so there'll be plenty of time for you to come up and have a noon meal. A big one, so there'll be enough leftovers to bring down here for supper. But I *was* thinking that breakfasts on weekends might be a problem, until . . . But look what I thought up." She opened the paper bag and showed them a dozen big glazed doughnuts, and beneath that a whole bunch of oranges.

As soon as Clarice opened the bag, Ursa dropped the rag he'd been playing with and came over to sit at the foot of the stairs, sniffing eagerly. Trixie and Buddy were right behind him. On his way to the stairs, Buddy was sniffing too. "What's in the bag, Clice?" he said.

"Breakfast." Clarice closed the bag, ran down the stairs to one of the tall cupboards, and put the bag way up on a high shelf. Buddy was right behind her, staring up at the bag. "Not right now," she told him. "It's for breakfast."

"Oh, breakfuss." Buddy sounded disappointed. "But it smells good right now."

Clarice laughed. "It will smell even better in the morning." To William and Jancy she added, "In the morning, just be sure to keep them quiet until you hear the car leave. That probably won't be until about ten thirty."

On the way up the stairs, headed for the kitchen and dinner, Jancy gave William a significant look. All he could do was shrug and nod. She was right. It was probably better that Clarice didn't know.

Dinner was tuna and noodles again. Apparently Clarice's lessons with her aunt's cook hadn't gotten much farther than roast chicken and tuna and noodles. After that there was the kitchen to clean up, a quick trip to the playroom to exchange toys, and then the four basement dwellers were herded back down to their hideout, just in time to hear the Ogdens' car rolling down the driveway.

Next came keeping the kids quiet until they finally got sleepy, putting them to bed, waiting for them to fall asleep, and then beginning to pack. After piling his own clothing on top of 𝕯oubleday's 𝕮omplete 𝖂orks of 𝖂illiam 𝖘hakespeare in his knapsack, William helped Jancy pack nearly everything else into the old leather suitcase.

While the two of them were packing, William was also doing some important planning. "I've been thinking," he said. "Once we get to Main Street we better go two by two. Like, Buddy with me, and Trixie with you. Pretending like we don't even know each other."

Jancy started to frown, but then she sighed and nodded. "Yeah, I get it," she said. "If there were posters about us, like Clarice said, and maybe something in the paper, too, it would have said there were four of us. Like . . ." She pretended to write a headline in the air. "'Four Baggett Kids Missing.' Right?"

"Right," William agreed. Jancy was nobody's fool. He got four dollars and twenty-five cents out of the bag that held his Getaway Fund and gave it to her. "Four dollars for two under-twelve-year-old tickets, and a little change, just in case," he said. "You can buy your own ticket and the one for Trixie. Okay?"

Jancy smoothed the dollars out on her knee and stared at them wide-eyed for a minute before she folded them carefully and put them in the little bag she used for a purse. She was looking excited and kind of proud. Probably it was the most money she'd ever held in her own hands, all at one time. "Okay," she said firmly. "I can do that."

So that much seemed to be decided, but there still was the problem of being sure to wake up early enough. But then Jancy came through again. Maybe? It seemed she'd been operating on the old alarm clock, and she thought she might have fixed it. "This morning, while you were gone, I opened up the back and connected a kind of lever thing that had come loose," she told William. "And then I set it for an hour later, and sure enough, it went off. Just like it used to. So now all we have to do is set it for six o'clock."

"And hope for the best," William said, secretly thinking they'd better not count on it. He'd simply do what he'd done before and force himself to stay awake all night. So he got into bed and started forcing himself, but without having had an afternoon nap, he wasn't too successful. The next thing he knew the alarm was going off, just like Jancy said it would, and it was six o'clock in the morning.

Before they got Trixie and Buddy up and dressed, they'd put the luggage outside the basement door, and Jancy had written the note explaining about the borrowed, not stolen, suitcase. Then at the last minute before waking Trixie and trying to wake Buddy, the oranges were peeled and the doughnut box invitingly opened. The doughnuts worked miracles. One sniff and old "dead-to-the-world" Buddy was wide awake, and then too busy eating doughnuts to even ask why. But when the doughnuts were all gone, the questions began.

"Why are we eating breakfuss down here?" That was Buddy, and then from Trixie, "Why can't we eat upstairs in the kitchen like before?" and then from the two of them, both at once and one at a time: "Where's Clarice?" from Trixie. "Where's Clice?" from Buddy. "Where's Ursa?" from both of them.

William decided it was time to try to explain, at least partly. To say, "This time we really are going to the Greyhound station, and then we'll go on a big bus to

Gold Beach. But we're going to have to leave very quietly like we did before."

Trixie looked anxious. "Like we did before? In the dark? I don't want to. I like it here. Why do we have to go?" she whimpered.

"It won't be in the dark because it's not as early as it was when we did it before," Jancy told her, but she only went on whimpering.

"Do I ride in the wagon like before?" Buddy wanted to know, and then before anyone could even try to answer, "Why not? Why can't I? Why are we going away, Willum?"

"Because I said so." William's growl sounded so Baggetty that it surprised everyone into sudden silence. Even William himself. He had to swallow hard and take a deep breath before he could add, "So come on now. We're leaving right this minute."

And they did, but not easily. For one thing, it turned out that the overstuffed leather suitcase was so heavy that, without help, skinny little Jancy could barely get it off the ground. So there went the plan to split up and go two by two, at least for the long walk down Gardenia Street. With his knapsack over one shoulder, William had a hand free to help out with the suitcase, but it was slow going. All the way down Gardenia they stopped to rest every few yards while Trixie and Buddy circled around them asking excited questions. The only good news was that there wasn't a single curious passerby around to watch and wonder, and maybe remember hearing something about four missing kids. Not a soul. People who lived on Gardenia Street, it seemed, didn't go out walking at six thirty in the morning.

But once they reached Main Street everything changed. By then bright sunlight was slanting over the horizon to the east, up and down Main Street a few cars were going by, and on the sidewalk there was an occasional pedestrian. Most of them were men dressed in overalls, who hurried by without even looking. But then a woman in a waitress's white cap and apron came to a stop. "What's this?" she demanded. "Where are you kids going? Where are your folks?"

Looking frantic, Jancy turned to William. "Hey, it's okay," he said, grinning. "Our car had a flat back there on Oak Street. Our dad is fixing it, but we have to get to the bus station and get them to wait. We have to hurry. Bye."

The waitress didn't look entirely convinced. She continued to frown, but she did step aside and let them pass. A few minutes more and they had reached Carson's Candy Store and the bus station was only two blocks away. But up ahead, where Orchard Street crossed Main, there were more people.

William pulled Jancy after him into the store's entryway, and put down the knapsack and the suitcase.

"Okay," he told Jancy, "here's where we really do have to split up. Do you think you can carry that thing the rest of the way by yourself?"

She nodded firmly. "I can," she said. "I will."

William grabbed Trixie and Buddy, one with each hand. "Now listen," he said. "Buddy is going with me, and Trixie will stay here with Jancy. Just for a little while, and then they'll come too. But when we see each other at the bus stop, we have to pretend we don't know each other. Buddy, you have to act like you don't even see Jancy and Trixie. Okay? Got it?"

Buddy's "Why?" sounded normal enough, but Trixie's was whimpery and fearful. "Why do you have to go first?" she said. "I don't want you to. I want you to stay with us."

"It's just for a while," William tried to explain. "We'll all be together again when we get to Gold Beach."

"But I want us all to be together always." Trixie was sobbing now. "I don't want William and Buddy to go without us."

But then Jancy whispered something in Trixie's ear, and Trixie nodded and sniffed, and Jancy went on whispering until Trixie wiped her eyes and began to smile. William never did find out exactly what Jancy said, but whatever it was, it worked. "Okay," she said to William. "You first. You guys get to have the first turn."

Throwing his knapsack over his shoulder, William

said, "Come on, Buddy," and started down the sidewalk, but Buddy stayed right where he was, looking back and forth from William to Jancy. He went on looking one way and then the other until Trixie gave him a shove, and after he'd shoved her back he trotted after William.

A small crowd of people was gathered around the door to the Greyhound ticket office, but William managed to push his way through with one hand while keeping the knapsack over his shoulder and his other hand around Buddy's wrist. At the counter he had to put the knapsack down and use both hands to get his money out of his pocket, but he kept checking to see if Buddy was still there. He was. Good. And the other good news was that the clerk was not the same guy who had seen William in his rich-kid costume. And this clerk didn't seem at all interested in who William and Buddy were, or whether they were with their parents.

So far so good, but when William finished buying the tickets and started to lead Buddy to the waiting area, he noticed that Buddy was stumbling along with one hand covering his eyes. When they got to a bench, William lifted Buddy up on it and pulled his hand away. He didn't seem to be crying, but when William pulled his hand away he put it right back. "What are you doing?" William asked. "Do your eyes hurt?"

Buddy shook his head. "No," he said. "I'm just not looking at Jancy and Trixie, like you said."

William couldn't help smiling. "Well, they aren't here yet, so you don't need to cover your eyes."

Buddy glanced around sneakily. "Not yet? When, Willum? When will they be here?"

"Pretty soon," William said. "Pretty soon they'll come in to buy their tickets, and that's when we have to pretend we don't know them. I'll tell you when."

Buddy nodded and put both his hands in his lap. But when William said, "They're coming now. They're going to the counter to buy their tickets," Buddy quickly put both hands over his eyes. William couldn't decide whether to laugh or groan.

When Jancy finished at the ticket counter, she and Trixie walked right past William and Buddy on their way to an empty bench, Jancy struggling with the heavy suitcase and Trixie with her head turned so far sideways that she looked like a painting on an Egyptian tomb. And Buddy still had his eyes covered. William decided that for the time being the best thing to do would be to ignore them, so he tried to concentrate on checking out the other people in the waiting area.

There were just five of them, and for the most part they didn't seem to be paying any special attention to him and Buddy, or to Jancy and Trixie, either. There was a youngish guy and a girl who were sitting close together and not looking at anyone except each other. No problem there. Then there were two older men. The one wearing a suit was reading the *Crownfield Daily*, and the guy in denim had his eyes shut most of the time. Probably all right, unless one or both or them had heard that the Crownfield police were looking for four missing kids.

The only person who seemed to be paying any attention to Jancy and Trixie was a grandmotherly-type woman, who stared at Trixie for a long time and then turned around to stare at Buddy.

William hoped it wasn't because she had any idea that they were the missing Baggetts. Not likely, he told himself. He could understand why she might stare at Trixie. People usually did until they were sure she wasn't really Shirley Temple. And as for Buddy, she was probably wondering why he had his hands over his eyes. He hoped that was all it was, anyway. He once again tried to pull Buddy's hands away from his eyes, but when Buddy glared at him and put them back up, he gave up and let them stay there—for the time being.

It probably wasn't quite half an hour, but it seemed like forever before a long blue and gray bus with the picture of the skinny dog on its side pulled up to the curb outside the ticket office.

William jumped up and, slinging his knapsack over his shoulder, dragged Buddy along behind him so fast they managed to be the first ones waiting on the curb. The bus was pretty full of mostly sleeping passengers, but there were some empty seats near the back, and that was where William headed. But it wasn't easy trying to hang on to Buddy's hand and at the same time avoid clobbering some sleeping passengers with the heavy lump 𝕾𝖍𝖆𝖐𝖊𝖘𝖕𝖊𝖆𝖗𝖊'𝖘 𝕮𝖔𝖒𝖕𝖑𝖊𝖙𝖊 𝖂𝖔𝖗𝖐𝖘 made at the bottom of his knapsack.

Once he'd lifted Buddy onto the seat and stored his bag under it, the first thing he did was look out the window to see how Jancy and Trixie were doing. He was worried about the leather suitcase. There was no way Jancy was going to be able to lift it up onto the bus by herself. But then a back door opened and the driver got on carrying a familiar brown suitcase, and put it on a rack near the door. Problem solved. And then there they were. Jancy and Trixie were coming down the aisle. And because the bus was so crowded, they kept coming until they reached the first empty seats—which turned out to be right across the aisle from William and Buddy.

Another case of not being able to decide whether to laugh or groan. On the one hand, it was kind of good to be able to keep an eye on them. But on the other, it wasn't going to be easy to make the sleeping passengers believe the four of them weren't together, when they woke up and saw them there, practically side by side. The most nerve-racking part was trying to guess what kind of a mess Trixie and Buddy were going to make of the situation.

It didn't take long to find out. Right at first it was just more of the same, with Buddy refusing to take his hands away from his eyes, and Trixie, who had the aisle seat, keeping her head turned sharply away. Leaning forward, William caught Jancy's eye and did a quick shrug and grin, and Jancy grinned back. The whole thing would have been funny if it hadn't been happening for such an unfunny reason.

As the bus started up and turned off Main Street onto Orchard, both Jancy and William got busy whispering to the little kids. William didn't know what Jancy was telling Trixie, but what he said to Buddy was, "Look, Buddy. Look at me. Take your hands down. Good. What we have to do now is just not talk to Jancy and Trixie. It's all right to look at them a little. Just don't stare at them for a long time or say anything to them. Nothing at all. Okay?"

Buddy was frowning. "Why?" he said.

William couldn't help grinning. For once it was a more or less necessary question. But not one that would be easy to answer so a four-year-old could understand it. "Well," he began, "it's this way. We don't ever want to go back to live with Big Ed and Gertie. Do we?"

Buddy frowned and shook his head back and forth. Slowly at first but then harder. "No," he said. "They hit me. Gertie hits me when I wet the bed. Big Ed hit me real bad when I kicked his beer over. I didn't mean to kick it, Willum."

"I know you didn't mean to." William was trying to keep his voice down to a low whisper. "So what we have to do is go live with our aunt in a town called Gold Beach."

"I know that," Buddy said. "With our ant in Gold

Beach." His smooth, round forehead puckered into a worried frown. "Is our ant a red one? Red ants bite you."

"Not that kind of ant," William said. "There are two kinds of aunts, Buddy. One is a little bug with six legs that lives in a hole in the ground—"

"And bites," Buddy interjected.

"Okay. And bites. But the other kind is a woman who's the sister of your dad or mom. Our mother was Aunt Fiona's sister. Got it?"

Buddy nodded a little uncertainly. "Maybe," he said. "Maybe I got it."

"Sure you do. You and Trixie lived with her until you were two years old. And Trixie was four. You don't remember, but Trixie does, and she says it was real nice there. But Big Ed wants to get all of us back, so he's told people to watch for us so he can come and take all *four* of us kids back. Four of us. Two little kids and two big ones."

Buddy thought that over and said, "I'm a big one."

"Okay, you're pretty big, all right. But now listen. Four kids." William held up Buddy's hand and counted on his fingers. "You and Trixie and Jancy and me. One, two, three, four. Got it?"

Buddy nodded.

"So we have to pretend we're not four kids from the same family." He separated the fingers—two and two.

"We're pretending we're just two kids and two different kids from somewhere else and we don't even know each other. So people who see us won't tell Big Ed they saw four of us on our way to Gold Beach. Okay?"

Buddy's eyes opened wide, and he smiled trium-phantly. "O-k-a-y," he drawled, and then nodded firmly. "I got it."

Whew! Big success. It looked like one more obstacle overcome—maybe. Knowing Buddy, it was hard to say for sure. But as time went by and the bus chugged along through the outskirts of Crownfield, and then out onto the highway between orchards and fields, Buddy went on acting like he really understood, talking to William and asking "Why?" a lot as usual, but not trying to say anything at all to Jancy and Trixie. And then he began to nod and went to sleep. When William risked a peek across the aisle, he saw that Trixie was sleeping too. Stealing a quick glance at Jancy, William raised his eyebrows and rolled his eyes in a "big relief" expression, and Jancy did it back.

William was half asleep himself, when the bus pulled into another station and stopped. "Okay everybody," the driver was shouting. "Here we are in Harrisford. We'll be here for about half an hour. Nice little café right next door to the station. A good place for a quick breakfast, you people who got on in Los Angeles."

While nearly all the other passengers were getting to

their feet, William sat tight, pretending to be still asleep. But then Buddy was poking him and saying, "Wake up, Willum. That bus driver said breakfuss."

Opening his eyes, William said loudly, loud enough for Trixie to hear too, "He didn't mean us. He meant all the people who've been on the bus since last night. We haven't. We've already had breakfast. Remember? Remember the doughnuts?"

Buddy shook his head. "Not very much," he said. "I don't remember them very much."

William checked up and down the aisle. The only other passenger still on the bus was the old lady who had been so interested in Trixie and Buddy back in the Crownfield station, and she seemed to be asleep.

Putting his hand in front of his mouth, William whispered sideways in Jancy's direction. "You still got some money?"

"Yes," Jancy whispered back.

"Okay. I'm going to take Buddy into the restroom and then I'll buy him something. Wait a minute and then you guys can come in too. Okay?"

So that's what they did. The little café right next to the station was packed with bus passengers. After a quick trip to the restroom, they made their way to the counter, where William ordered two strawberry ice-cream cones.

He and Buddy were on their way out the door just as Jancy and Trixie came in, which, for a moment, put a big strain on the effort to ignore each other. Trixie was goggle-eyed. Ice-cream cones didn't happen at the Baggetts. She stared at Buddy's cone and his gloating, strawberry-smeared face. Before the door swung shut behind them, William heard the beginning of a typical Trixie whimper. But right at that moment William saw something that wiped the grin off his face.

Leaning against a streetlight pole, smoking a cigarette, was a guy whose pimply face, ducktail hairdo, and wide-legged, floppy pants looked vaguely familiar. Looked like he might be someone William had seen before and wouldn't have wanted to see again under any circumstances, but particularly not now. A guy who was, at the moment, staring hard—at William and Buddy.

Turning his face away from the strangely familiar-looking guy with the weird hairdo, William hustled Buddy back onto the bus and down the aisle to their seat. As soon as Buddy had finished his ice-cream cone, licked his fingers, stuck his tongue way out, and ran it as far as it would go around his face, William began to question him. "Buddy, did you see the guy in the floppy pants leaning against the post in front of the café?"

After some thought, Buddy said, "Maybe. Maybe I saw him."

"The one smoking a cigarette," William urged. "Did he look familiar to you?"

"Familer?" Buddy asked.

"Like someone you might have seen before?"

Buddy nodded. "Maybe I did before. I don't like him before."

William almost gasped. "How do you know you don't like him?"

"He played too hard. He played box fight so hard it made me cry."

"He did? When? When did he play with you?"

"Rudy let him," Buddy said. "Rudy just laughed, but it hurt me real bad. Right on my nose. It made me cry."

William swallowed hard. It was just what he'd been afraid of. The guy with the baggy pants must be one of Rudy's lousy friends. And if he was, he must have been staring at them because he recognized them and probably knew that they were the missing Baggett kids. And now he was going to tell Big Ed where he saw them. And Big Ed would know where they were going for sure, because the bus was headed for Reedly—just a few miles from Gold Beach.

William hoped, hoped desperately, that he wasn't right about that, but he was afraid he was. It took a few minutes of mindless panic for him to settle down enough to start making new plans, or change the ones he'd already made, to deal with the possibility that the guy was going to squeal on them to Big Ed.

Okay, he asked himself, *when is he going to tell Big Ed? How soon?*

Since phone service to the Baggetts had been cut off weeks ago, there probably wasn't any way the guy could do his squealing until he got back to Crownfield. So how soon depended on where the guy was going, and how long it would be before he would be back in the Crownfield area where he could talk to Rudy and Big Ed in person. So the best news would be if he was going to stay on the bus for a long time, like all the way to Oregon, if the bus was going that far.

However, William's next thought went in a different direction. Maybe it didn't matter all that much, because Big Ed must already have guessed where they would be going. After all, where else could they go? And maybe he'd already gone to Gold Beach, while the four of them were still in the Ogdens' basement. And if he had, he'd have found out that Aunt Fiona hadn't seen them and didn't know where they were.

In that case, the only way that guy could mess things up was if he told the Baggetts exactly *when* he'd seen William and Buddy. Because then Big Ed would guess that they were going to show up at Aunt Fiona's after all, just a little later than he'd expected them to.

The whole scene was terribly complicated and pretty scary, and it got even more so when the passengers began getting back on the bus and one of them was the familiar-looking tall, skinny guy with baggy pants and a mean grin. A grin that he definitely aimed right at William as he was starting down the aisle to his seat. William tried to put on an "I got nothing to worry about" grin, right back at him, but he didn't think it came off very well.

For the next hour or so, while the bus headed north and then west, there was nothing William could do but worry. He kept wishing he could talk to Jancy about Rudy's mean friend and find out how much of a problem she thought he might turn out to be. But of course he couldn't. Meanwhile Buddy had a lot to say about doughnuts and ice-cream cones and which he liked best and which one William liked best—and, of course, why?

It was more than an hour later and the sun was pretty high in the sky before the bus stopped again. "This is the end of the line for those of you going to Summerford," the driver said. "Just a restroom stop for the rest of you. Be back on the bus in fifteen minutes."

In that case, William thought, he'd just as soon not get off and run the chance of coming face-to-face with Rudy's pal, which might just remind him to do something about having discovered where the runaway Baggetts were. Remind him maybe to do something right away, and since he couldn't call and tell Rudy, perhaps he'd think the next best thing would be to tell the Summerford police. It was a frightening thought. The only thing that made that idea a little less alarming was the definite possibility that the baggy pants guy was the type of person who, like his Baggett friends, always kept as far away from the police as possible. A likely possibility, William told himself hopefully.

Meanwhile Buddy was tugging at his sleeve and

saying he wanted to get off. And when William turned the tables on him and asked him, "Why?" he thought for a minute before he announced that he needed to go to the bathroom. What he actually said sounded like a question. "'Cause I need to go to the baffroom?"

William wasn't sure if the question was whether he really needed to go, or whether William was going to believe him if he said he did. But knowing Buddy, he thought he'd better not risk it, so they got off the bus. And of course, a minute or two later Jancy and Trixie got off too. Trixie wasn't one to let anybody else have a privilege—and maybe an ice-cream cone—that she didn't get in on.

The whole scene might have been kind of amusing, except that there he was again—Rudy's weird-looking friend—standing on the sidewalk and staring at William and Buddy as they entered the station. And what happened next might turn out to be even more worrisome.

The scary thing was, when they came out of the men's room the guy was gone. He wasn't there in the bus station, nor was he one of the people who got back on the bus. Which meant that the only person who knew where the missing Baggett kids were had gotten off the bus in the little town of Summerford, where he might be making a short visit and then going back to Crownfield, which was only about sixty-five miles away. Not a very comforting thought.

The rest of the trip to Reedly was only about thirty-five miles, according to the map William had picked up at the bus station, but it seemed an awful lot longer. Having to make conversation on a four-year-old level while trying to figure out the best way to get from Reedly to Gold Beach as quickly as possible, as well as wondering what kind of welcome they might expect once they got there, made for an effort that was pretty exhausting, especially after Buddy decided that he wanted to hear a story.

"What story? I don't know any stories," William said.

"Yes, you do. You did a story at Clice's house. The one about setting everything on fire."

"But that wasn't the sort of story you can just tell. You have to run around and act it out. And I can't do that here."

"Why not?" Buddy said.

William snorted and made a gesture with both arms. "Because, look, there's no room. You can't run around in a bus."

"Oh." Buddy seemed to get the picture. But then he added, "But you could sing it. There's enough room to sing it."

William considered the request. There really hadn't been any singing in act one of 𝕮𝕳𝖊 𝕿𝖊𝖒𝖕𝖊𝖘𝖙. However, in act four . . . That's how it happened that William sang his favorite Ariel song all the way through twice, on the way to Reedly. Sang it just the way he'd done in the play, only not nearly as loudly.

"𝔚here the bee sucks, there suck 𝔍:/𝔍n a cowslip's bell 𝔍 lie;/𝔗here 𝔍 couch when owls do cry./𝔒n the bat's back 𝔍 do fly/ 𝔄fter summer merrily./𝔐errily, merrily shall 𝔍 live now/𝔘nder the blossom that hangs on the bough.'"

He sang so softly he thought no one except Buddy could hear, but when he finished, a gray-haired man and woman who were seated just in front of them clapped softly, then turned around and stared.

William couldn't help grinning and taking a little bow, even though he knew it was a dangerous thing to have done. Like, what if those gray-haired people had heard about the Baggett kid who'd been such a hit last year in Crownfield High's 𝔖hakespeare production—*and then had gone missing*? All he could do was hope they were from Los Angeles and had never heard of William Baggett or Crownfield High, and just happened to like 𝔖hakespeare. In the meantime, Buddy seemed about to go back to sleep.

At long last they passed a sign that said it was just two miles to Reedly, and there began to be stores and gas stations instead of just open fields. And then finally they made a left turn and pulled up in front of a Greyhound bus station. So they were almost to the end of their journey. But what William knew only too well was that what was left was the three or four miles between Reedly and Gold Beach. And he wasn't at all sure just how he would get himself and Jancy, two little kids and two big pieces of luggage, the rest of the way there.

Well, here we are in the fine little city of Reedly," the bus driver was announcing. "For you passengers going on north, this will be your lunch stop. There's a good little coffee shop just down the street to my left. For those of you who are leaving us here, be sure to check under your seats for any personal belongings."

This time William motioned to Jancy that she and Trixie should get off first, and by the time he and Buddy reached the front of the bus, the driver had retrieved the big suitcase from the rack and delivered it to Jancy. "Here you are, little lady," he was saying while William was still helping Buddy down the bus's steep steps. "Hope you're going to have some help getting this heavy thing all the way home."

"Oh, I am," Jancy told him. "We're visiting my aunt, and she'll take care of everything." Jancy had always been good at telling a thing in a way that made it not quite a real lie, and worked just as well.

William, with Buddy in tow, continued to keep a certain distance from Jancy and Trixie, until the other passengers had pretty much dispersed, most of them heading toward the coffee shop the bus driver had pointed out. But then he sidled closer. Close enough to say, "Well, here we are."

He got a three-way response—three questions, almost in unison. Trixie said, "Where's Aunt Fiona?" Jancy asked, "Where are the taxicabs?" And from Buddy, "Where's lunch?" But then he added, almost apologetically, "That bus man said lunch stop. I heard him say it."

Typical Buddy, but this time he might be right. It was well past midday, and except for ice-cream cones and that very early doughnut breakfast, they hadn't had anything to eat all day. And it would be best not to arrive at Aunt Fiona's as hungry as a bunch of stray dogs.

But could they afford it? There still had to be around twenty-some dollars in his Getaway Fund, which would probably be more than enough for the taxicab to Gold Beach. So maybe they could afford lunch, as long as it wasn't too expensive.

William looked around. On the block to his right were several small stores, including the coffee shop the driver had pointed out. Not there, William thought. Better to let all those other passengers, particularly the ones from Crownfield, forget about the four kids who'd been on their bus.

Down the sidewalk the other way, you could see what seemed to be the main part of town. Some bigger stores came first—a JCPenney department store and a Sears, Roebuck—and then just beyond Sears, another café where a bright neon sign said ELMER'S EATERY.

"Do you think it would be all right for us to go to lunch together?" Jancy was asking. "All four of us?"

Trixie was doing her tiptoes thing. "Yes, yes please. All of us together?"

William thought it over for a minute before he shrugged. "I guess it would be all right." Chances were that way up here in Reedly no one had heard anything about the Baggetts and their missing kids. "Yeah, I guess we can go together," he said.

But there was still the luggage problem. Would a restaurant nice enough to have a fancy flashing neon sign let people come in dragging a huge leather suitcase and a bulgy knapsack? Probably not. He'd gotten that far in his thinking when, as if a neon sign had been flashing on his forehead, saying, LUGGAGE PROBLEM, LUGGAGE PROBLEM, Jancy said, "Maybe we could leave it here. In the ticket office." Another example of the sort of mind-reading thing Jancy was so good at—reading William's mind, at any rate.

A few minutes later, with the knapsack and suitcase safely stored away by the friendly ticket clerk, all four of them were entering the nicest restaurant any of them had ever been in. Well, actually the only restaurant they'd ever been in—except for William himself, of course. Since Miss Scott and the whole cast of 𝕿𝖍𝖊 𝕿𝖊𝖒𝖕𝖊𝖘𝖙 had gone out to eat three times—two lunches and a closing-day banquet—William was pretty experienced at that sort of thing.

Elmer's was the kind of place where there were cloth napkins on the tables, and waitresses in white aprons. As a friendly waitress led them to a table, William made an effort to look relaxed and self-confident, but with Trixie walking on tiptoe and Buddy staring at everything goggle-eyed, his cool, worldly-wise role was a little hard to hang on to. After they were all seated, with a fancy high chair for Buddy, came the problem of ordering from a menu where everything was shockingly expensive, with even a hamburger sandwich costing an incredible twenty-five cents.

But it wasn't as if he didn't have the money. Without too much soul-searching, William wound up ordering four hamburgers and four milk shakes. He hated to see that much of his hard-earned money disappear, but it was, he tried to convince himself, worth it. And the stunned expressions on the kids' faces, when all the food arrived on a big tray that the waitress carried expertly, way up high over her shoulder, made him almost forget about the expense.

With Trixie and Buddy concentrating on their

hamburgers and milk shakes, there was a chance for William and Jancy to have a serious discussion about what was going to happen next. William grinned at Jancy and, just as a joke, began by saying, "You know it's not as far from here to Gold Beach as it was from the Baggett's to Crownfield. We could walk it, if we had that old three-wheeled wagon of yours to put the luggage in."

Jancy didn't seem to be in the mood for kidding around. "It wasn't mine, and we don't," she said coldly. "I thought you said we could go the rest of the way by taxicab."

He nodded. "Yeah, I said that, and I guess we can. It'll be expensive, but I'm pretty sure I have enough."

"Pretty sure?" Jancy asked sharply. "I thought you said you had plenty."

"Oh, I do," he reassured her. "I've got plenty. It's just that I hate . . ."

He kind of ran down then, but Jancy the mind reader finished the thought for him.

"You just hate to part with your precious getaway money, I guess."

He grinned sheepishly. She was right, he supposed. He remembered how he used to make the dangerous trip, slithering down over the crossbeams in the attic, even when he didn't have anything to add to his Getaway Fund. Just to stack up his nickels and dimes and count them, like a miser counting his gold. It was an embarrassing thought.

"Yeah, you're right," he told Jancy. "We'll go by taxicab."

But then, back at the Greyhound ticket office, he found out that his generous offer wasn't going to get them anywhere. There wasn't a single taxi in the whole town of Reedly.

"Not anymore," the clerk told them. "Used to be Tony Martinez had a license, but then his old cab broke down and he quit. Where is it you kids want to go?"

It was Jancy who answered. "To Gold Beach," she said. "We're going to our aunt's house in Gold Beach."

The ticket clerk, a tall man with a kind of Shakespearean-type beard, almost like Prospero's in the Rockwell Kent illustration, rubbed his fuzzy chin while he peered over the counter at the four of them. At Buddy, who was leaning against William's leg and staring up at him wide-eyed, and Trixie, who was giving him her cutest Shirley Temple smile. "You know what?" he said. "I live in Gold Beach, and if you kids can wait a couple of hours till I get off, I can take you there. If you don't mind riding in a beat-up old Model A."

Of course they didn't mind, and for a while it looked like their troubles, as far as getting to Aunt Fiona's house anyway, were pretty much over. Of course, there was still the chance that they wouldn't be welcome when they got there, but that possibility was one that William had been trying hard not to worry about. They'd cross that bridge, he kept telling himself, when they came to it.

So that was the way things were, and for the moment the only problem seemed to be keeping Trixie and Buddy from punching each other while they waited for almost two hours on the hard wooden bench in the ticket office.

But it was then, right there in the bus station, that another serious problem started to develop. It began, for William at least, when he noticed that Jancy was pawing around in the little crocheted bag she used as a purse. Pawing around, taking things out and putting them back, and finally dumping everything onto the bench. As far as William could see, there wasn't much—only a broken comb, a stubby pencil, a handkerchief, a quarter, two dimes, and a penny—and what looked like a badly wrinkled envelope. And when William asked what she was looking for, she only gasped and said, "I know I put it in here. I know it. But now it's gone."

Holding up the wrinkled envelope, she said, "See. Here's the other one. But the one that had her address on it just isn't here." She paused long enough to shake her head slowly from side to side, before she wailed, "And I can't remember what her address was."

"I don't believe it," William whispered, trying not to sound too frantic. "You wrote Aunt Fiona all those letters and you don't remember what the address was?"

"I wrote her *three* letters," Jancy said coldly. "A long time ago. And she only answered the first two. And only the first one had her address on it. After that she gave me this post office box number." Jancy held up the one wrinkled envelope. "See there. Just a post office box number. I know I still had both letters. But the other one's just disappeared. I've looked and looked."

"The street name," William urged. "Can't you even remember the name of the street?" He was thinking that if they knew the street, they could make up a house number to tell the ticket clerk and have him drop them there. And then, after he drove off, they could walk up and down the street until . . . Well, until something happened. Maybe Trixie would recognize the house, or Aunt Fiona would just happen to come out and find them.

Jancy closed her eyes tightly and rocked her head from side to side. Trixie and Buddy stopped poking each other and watched her. "Why is Jancy doing this?" Buddy said, rocking his head back and forth.

"She's thinking," William said. "She's trying to remember the name of the street where Aunt Fiona lives." Another possibility occurred to him, not a very likely one, perhaps. After all, she'd only been four years old when she left. But worth a try.

Grabbing Trixie's shoulder, he gave it a shake to be sure he had her full attention. "Listen, Trixie," he said. "I don't suppose you can remember the name of the street. The street where you lived with Aunt Fiona."

"Oh," Trixie said. "I think I can. I'll think about it."

She rocked her head back and forth the way Jancy had been doing, before she said triumphantly, "I do remember. Sort of. I remember it was a name."

"Not funny," William said sarcastically, and turned back to Jancy. But she only shook her head sadly. Right at that moment the ticket clerk came out from behind the counter and said, "Okay, kids, follow me. We're off to Gold Beach."

Just as he'd said, the ticket agent's Model A was pretty beat up, with rusty running boards and lots of dents, but, as it turned out, it did have one redeeming feature: a rumble seat. A leather-covered backseat that opened up behind the cab, so it would be almost like riding in a convertible. William had never ridden in a rumble seat and neither, of course, had the other kids, but they all, including William himself, immediately wanted to. This was a development that, along with finding room for their luggage, made things a little complicated.

It took several minutes of discussion and a little whimpering and whining before it was decided that the two little kids and Jancy would ride in the rumble seat. Which meant that only William, along with the suitcase and knapsack, would be in the cab with the driver. Which also meant that it was going to be up to him, all by himself, to decide what to tell the ticket clerk about where he should let them out.

Fortunately, the Model A turned out to be in such bad condition, with lots of jerky starts and stops and sudden motor deaths, that the helpful ticket clerk was too busy keeping it going to think about asking exactly where they were headed until they were almost there.

They stopped and started, died and revived, and finally coasted in neutral down a steep, curvy road with a nice view of the ocean. Or at least the clerk said there was a nice view. Because of being buried under all the luggage, William wasn't able to see much. It wasn't until they were well within the outskirts of Gold Beach that the Model A's owner got around to asking William just where he should let them off.

In desperation, William had decided that he would say they wanted to be dropped off at the post office. And when the owner of the Model A wanted to know why, he would just say . . . what?

He'd almost composed a halfway sensible answer to that question when Jancy began to knock violently on the back window and yell something unintelligible, but that clearly included the word "STOP!" The driver slammed on the brakes, and the Ford came to such a quick stop that William might have gone right through the windshield if he hadn't been pinned down by so much luggage. Struggling to see around his knapsack, he tried to stay calm, even though his first guess was that someone, probably Buddy, had fallen onto the road.

He had to wait several more frantic moments while Jancy climbed out of the rumble seat and up onto the running board, stuck her head in the window, and said, "We're here. This is the street." She pointed triumphantly. "Right back there. Eleanor Street."

And when the ticket clerk asked if he should back up and drive down Eleanor, she said quickly, "No. You don't need to do that. The house is real close. We can walk the rest of the way."

They had all thanked the friendly owner of the rumble seat over and over again and waved good-bye until he had chugged and jolted out of sight, before William turned to Jancy and opened his mouth to say, "What in the world . . . ?" Jancy and Trixie, both at once, began to explain.

Jancy was saying, "I started reading the street names out loud as soon as we got to Gold Beach, and as soon as I said Eleanor, Trixie screamed, 'That's it!' And then I remembered too. That was the street name on the envelope that got lost."

And at the same time Trixie was saying, "See, William, I did remember. Just like I told you. As soon as Jancy read that sign"—she stopped long enough to point—"that sign right over there that says 'Eleanor,' I remembered that was it. And it *was so* a name, just like I told you. I just didn't remember whose name it was."

Another big problem more or less solved. But still . . .

William sighed. That still left the biggest one—the one problem that he'd been trying to push out of his mind ever since they'd decided to run away. And that was what their aunt was going to do when they appeared on her doorstep. An imagined scene that he'd been trying to pull the curtain on every time it shoved its way into his consciousness. A scene in which Aunt Fiona took one look at four hungry, bedraggled runaway Baggetts and slammed the door in their faces.

After all, you could hardly blame her. How many people would be willing to take in four kids—two little ones she hadn't seen for two years, plus an eleven-year-old and an almost teenager whom she'd barely met—to feed and clothe, and probably have to hide from an angry Ed Baggett? Who would be willing to do such a thing? William's best guess was that the answer to that question had to be, *nobody in their right mind.*

But whatever the answer was going to be, it was beginning to look like they were going to get it very soon. Sure enough, as soon as they started down Eleanor Street, Trixie began to remember some other things. "Look," she was saying. "Hey, Buddy. Look at that house with the big fence around it. Remember the great big police dog who used to bark at us? Remember?" And then, while Buddy was still shaking his head, "Look! Look! There he is."

And he certainly was. A big, mean-looking German shepherd was running across the lawn, barking fiercely.

William and Jancy and Buddy, too, were backing away, but Trixie was saying, in a soothing, grownup-sounding voice, "It's all right, kiddos. He's a bad dog all right, but it's a good, strong fence. Just don't ever put your fingers through the wire."

"Is that what Aunt Fiona said?" Jancy asked, and Trixie nodded, looking very pleased with herself. But when William once again asked her which was Aunt Fiona's house, she still didn't seem sure. She looked back and forth down the street several times and then pointed. "This way, I think. Maybe it's down this way."

And so William and Jancy changed hands on the heavy suitcase and knapsack and struggled on down Eleanor Street. They had passed several more houses, including one with a fancy fountain that Trixie thought she remembered, when they came to an old-fashioned wooden house with a wide front porch, and Trixie once again came to a stop. "I think that's our house. Remember, Buddy? Isn't that where we lived? Yes, yes. That's it."

Then, before anyone could even try to stop her, she was running up the walk, climbing the steps, and ringing the doorbell, while Buddy was still shaking his head and saying, "I don't think I live there."

What with carrying all the luggage and waiting while Buddy put one foot and then the other on every one of the steep stairs, William and Jancy had barely arrived on the porch when the door opened, and there she was.

There was a slender woman with lots of brown hair who, right at first, didn't look especially familiar to William. Except there was something about her that brought back a tumbled rush of mixed-up memories—good ones and bad ones. Memories of the way he'd felt about his quiet, gentle mother, and how it had become mixed with resentment when she didn't stand up for him the way he felt she should have. The same kind of resentment he knew he was going to feel when this halfway familiar person did what she was surely going to do—point her finger, stamp her foot, and tell them to go away and stop messing up her nice, quiet life.

But then, after staring and gasping for a long second, Aunt Fiona dropped to her knees and reached out and grabbed Trixie, who still had her finger on the doorbell, and Buddy, too. "Oh, thank God," she almost sobbed. "You're all right? You are all right." And then, looking up at William and Jancy, she demanded, "But where were you? Where on earth have you been?"

At first William didn't understand what Aunt Fiona was raving about, but by the time she led the way down the hall and into a big, good-smelling kitchen, she'd pretty much explained. It seemed that just two days before, on Thursday, Big Ed and two of his full-grown sons had shown up at her front door. Three big, angry, threatening men, who pushed their way right past her into her house, demanding that she give back their kids.

"They told me all four of you had disappeared several days before and nobody had seen you since, and they were sure that you must have come here. But of course you weren't here, and I hadn't heard a word from you. But when I tried to tell them so, they wouldn't believe me. They insisted on going through the whole house, looking in all the closets and under beds and even in cupboards, before they finally gave up and went away." She sighed again, grabbed Buddy, and picked him up—a stiff, startled-looking Buddy—and hugged him hard as she asked William, "Where *have* you been all this time?"

"We were on our way here," William started to explain, "but we kind of stopped off for a few days at a . . . well, at a friend's house, and . . ."

"But couldn't you have phoned?" Aunt Fiona frowned at William and then at Jancy. Buddy was pushing her arms away, struggling to get down. "I've been so worried since I heard you were missing. I've been imagining all sorts of terrible things that might have happened to you."

"I guess we could have phoned," William said. "We should have, but we didn't know your phone number. And besides . . ." He paused, wondering if it would be all right to say what he was thinking, but then Jancy interrupted and said it for him.

Jancy flat-out told Aunt Fiona, "We were afraid that if we did, you'd tell us not to come." Tears were flooding Jancy's big eyes, and her chin was beginning to quiver as she went on, "And we didn't have anywhere else in the whole world to go."

For a moment Aunt Fiona stared from Jancy to William and back again, before she put Buddy down and grabbed them both at once and hugged them. And it was right then, with Aunt Fiona's arms around him and Jancy, that William began to let himself start to believe, just a little bit, that maybe this running-away thing might turn out all right after all. Still a pretty big maybe, because of the Baggett problem—the possibility a bunch of Baggetts might show up again at any moment to take them back. But there would be time to worry about that later.

Right at the moment all he could think was how completely different everything seemed now that he'd met Aunt Fiona and was beginning to understand what she was really like. And to see how her old house with its shiny wood floors and good-smelling kitchen looked, smelled, and just plain felt so different from any of the places he'd ever lived as a Baggett.

"𝕺 brave new world,/that has such people in't," William found himself thinking, one of his favorite lines from 𝕿𝖍𝖊 𝕿𝖊𝖒𝖕𝖊𝖘𝖙, but one that, up until that moment, he'd never found much use for.

But now Aunt Fiona was saying to them, "Well, and so here you are, and I'm so glad to really meet both of you, at last." She took a deep breath and shook her head slowly from side to side before she went on. "There's so much to talk about and make plans for, but I guess what we should do first and foremost is decide what we can do about dinner, and where you all are going to sleep tonight, and—"

"We won't take up a lot of room," Jancy said quickly.

"No, we won't at all." Trixie was bouncing up and down again and doing her dimpled smile. "At Clarice's house, Buddy and me slept in just one little old cot, and we didn't even kick each other. Not very much, anyway."

And then Buddy got into the act by announcing proudly, "And I didn't wet the bed, either. Not even once." Which for some reason made Aunt Fiona pick him up and hug him again.

"I just can't believe you," she told him. "You've gotten to be so big, and you're talking like a grownup. You're not my little baby anymore, are you?" She kind of nuzzled her face against Buddy's neck. "Don't you remember when you were my baby, Buddy?"

"No." Buddy shook his head solemnly. "I don't remember." But he had stopped pushing her away and trying to get down. Instead he put one arm around Aunt Fiona's neck and said, "I don't remember, but maybe I'm going to."

So then Aunt Fiona got out some pasta and sausages and added them to the good-smelling stuff that she was already cooking. And all the time she was cooking and setting the table for four more people, and later, when they were eating, she was talking and asking questions.

While they were still at the table, they told her about how they'd hidden in the basement at the Ogdens' house, and how Clarice had scared them into staying longer when they wanted to leave, by saying the police were looking for them, when they really weren't.

And when Aunt Fiona wondered why Clarice had done that, William quickly said, "I think it was just because she's a lonely person and she liked having some people around to talk to for a change." Then he frowned at Jancy and said firmly, "That's what I think, anyway." Jancy got the message. She grinned slightly and ducked her head, but she kept her mouth shut.

It wasn't until later that evening, after the little kids had been put to bed, that Auntie—she'd said they could call her Auntie when they felt like it—began to tell William and Jancy about the day Ed Baggett came and took Buddy and Trixie away.

"It was the worst day of my life," she told them. Her lips were quivering as she went on, "I'd had those two beautiful babies since right after Laura, your mother, died. Ever since Buddy was just a week old, and Trixie was only a toddler. I'd really come to think of them as my own. I never imagined for a minute that Ed would ever want them back, and then . . ." She stopped, shaking her head and biting her lip for a long moment, before she went on. "I never liked Ed Baggett. I had always been so terribly sorry Laura married him. But on that day I hated that man so much. . . ."

She sighed and stopped again, and then Jancy brought up something that William had wondered about for a long time. Like always, Jancy was good at saying straight out what she was thinking about. "I wonder why our mama married Big Ed. I was only six when she died, but I remember her pretty well. She was always good to us, or at least she tried to be, except sometimes when Big Ed was around, and she could only do just what he told her to." Jancy shook her head and sighed. "I guess she was afraid of him, like everybody else."

"I know. I've always wondered too," Auntie said. "It's a complicated story. After Laura graduated from high school, she went to live with some cousins of ours in Crownfield, because the junior college there had such a good drama department. Laura was such a pretty girl, and she'd always wanted to be an actress."

Jancy looked at William with raised eyebrows, and guessing what the eyebrows were suggesting, he grinned back at her and nodded—a nod that meant something about acting talent and where it might have come from.

But Aunt Fiona went right on. "I guess you know that the Crownfield schools have always had exceptional drama departments. Anyway, Laura was going to the college, but she was also doing some community service helping out families who were having difficulties, and somehow she got acquainted with Mabel Baggett. You know, Ed Baggett's first wife—the mother of the first six kids. The oldest one was—"

"Little Ed," Jancy offered.

Auntie nodded. "Yes. Ed Junior was only about six years old, and there were three others before the twins, who were still infants when Mabel Baggett started having some kind of a nervous breakdown. She'd gotten to the point where she couldn't begin to take care of all those children, and Laura started helping her out. Laura always loved babies."

It was William's turn to raise an eyebrow and nod at Jancy. A nod that this time meant that being crazy about all sorts of little things might have come from the same place.

"And then Mabel Baggett disappeared. Left all her children, as well as Big Ed, and ran away back to wherever it was she came from."

"Didn't Big Ed even go look for her?" William asked.

"Yes. Laura said he did. At least he went off for several months, and Laura took care of the children while he was gone. But when he came back, Mabel wasn't with him, and he said he'd gotten a divorce. Laura had finished her second year at the junior college by then, and she just went on taking care of the kids for several more months, when for some reason she decided to marry Ed Baggett. Our father was still alive at that time, and both he and I tried to talk her out of it, but she wouldn't listen." Auntie shook her head and sighed. "And then you were born, William, and then Jancy."

"Did you ever go to see her?" Jancy asked.

"I tried," Auntie said. "But Ed made it clear that I wasn't welcome. I guess he knew what my father and I thought of him, and it made him angry. And when he was angry, he took it out on Laura."

The three of them sat there staring at each other for another minute or two before Aunt Fiona stood up and said, "It's late, and I know you must be very tired. Tomorrow we'll need to start making all sorts of plans, but in the meantime let's all go to bed."

And so they did, with Jancy and Trixie sharing one twin bed in what Aunt Fiona called her guest room, while Buddy had the other all to himself.

And William S. Baggett had a deep bath in a claw-foot bathtub and then went to bed in a small corner room that had been his mother's when she was a little girl. A room with a braided rug on a shiny wood floor, and snow-white curtains on the windows.

Even though Gold Beach wasn't quite as hot as Crownfield, it wasn't exactly cool in William's room that night. But then a breeze began to breathe through the open windows. Only a gentle, silent sigh, but enough to move the moonlit curtains in and out.

Stretched out on the clean, soft bed, William watched the drifting curtains and tried not to think too much about how good it all looked and felt— just in case. In case it didn't last, and he'd wake up to find himself back on the floor of a hot, smelly attic in a house full of Baggetts. Back there, where a clean, soft bed would be only a thing to dream about. To dream, and then wake up and say, like Caliban did in act three, **"when J waked,/J cried to dream again."**

The next morning, when his internal seven-thirty alarm went off, he awoke to the smell of coffee and bacon and hurried downstairs. And it was then, while he was helping Aunt Fiona with breakfast and the other kids weren't yet awake, the two of them started to face up to the Ed Baggett problem, and what might happen if he showed up again.

At first Aunt Fiona said she thought he just might not. "I really do believe that when he was here on Thursday, he went away convinced that I was telling the truth— that you kids weren't here and that I hadn't even known about your disappearance. Of course, he didn't bother to apologize for the three of them stomping around my house in their dirty boots, looking through all my closets and cupboards. But he did say something about how he'd guessed wrong, and he'd have to guess again."

"Did he say anything about the police?" William asked. "Like whether the police were looking for us?"

Aunt Fiona shook her head. "No. Not a thing." She stopped setting the table and just stood there for a long minute, biting her lip and shaking her head before she said, "He didn't say anything about having reported you missing to anybody. Actually, I really doubt if he had. Not at that point, at any rate."

William agreed. "Yeah. He probably thought he didn't need to, because he knew where we were, and he didn't need to hurry to come here and get us back. As long as it was before Mrs. Montgomery showed up again."

"Mrs. Montgomery?" Aunt Fiona asked.

William grinned ruefully. "She's the social worker who comes to check on how many kids need New Deal money."

Then too, there was that other reason William could believe that Big Ed had never reported them missing. That was how sure he now was that Clarice had made up all that stuff about police cars and posters. Made it all up, just to keep him—keep all four of them, that is—from trying to catch the bus for Gold Beach.

There was also the fact that if you knew anything at all about Big Ed, you'd know he absolutely never talked to policemen, except when they started it.

But still, when his aunt said, "So maybe, if we're lucky, we've seen the last of Ed Baggett," William felt he had to tell her that he did have one kind of scary reason to believe they probably weren't going to be that lucky.

What he had to say was, "Well, maybe, but the thing is, I think there was a guy on the bus yesterday who used to hang around with Rudy and Little Ed. One of their deadbeat friends, who's been to the house at least once. I think he probably recognized all of us, especially Buddy. Buddy said he teased him and kind of hurt him. On the bus the guy stared at us, but he didn't say anything. And then he got off in Summerford."

"Oh dear." Aunt Fiona had a way of pressing her open right hand against her cheek when she was worried, and she was doing that now. "So you're thinking that he'll tell them that he saw you on your way here, but not until yesterday. Not until after they'd already been here looking for you. Oh dear."

Watching how worried and frightened she was looking, William had a sinking feeling that she was going to say they couldn't stay after all. That she just couldn't face having Ed Baggett come stomping back into her house and find his kids here, after all. But then she took a deep breath and said, "Well, I guess we'd better start thinking of a way to handle things if and when they show up again." She smiled and then sighed. "Like finding a foolproof hiding place where we can put all four of you and make everything look as if you were never here."

William was amazed. What popped into his mind at that moment was, once again, the **"brave new world"** quote, but all he said was, "Yeah, that's a good idea. Do you think we can?"

They started working on finding a hiding place that same morning. Jancy helped, but the little kids, who were trying to do pick-up sticks on the kitchen table, weren't in on it at all.

The three of them, William and Jancy and Aunt Fiona, went through the upstairs first, looking in all three bedrooms and the bath, but except for the closets and under the beds, places where the Baggetts had looked before and were sure to look again, there didn't seem to be any possibilities. But then Aunt Fiona came up with an interesting suggestion. Way at the back of her bedroom closet was a little square door that led into a very shallow attic area, where the roof went out over the back porch. With longish dresses hanging in front of it, you didn't even see the little door when you opened the closet, and the Baggetts apparently hadn't noticed it when they were there before. The area was packed full of cardboard cartons of stored-away stuff, but after the boxes were removed, there just might be enough room for four tightly-squeezed-together kids.

So they cleared it out, with William crawling in and handing out the boxes, and Aunt Fiona contributing some old quilts to pad the rough, unfinished floor. Then came showing it to the little kids and explaining what it was for—and why. Auntie thought it might frighten Trixie and Buddy too much if they really knew why they had to practice hiding. So when they took the kids up to show them the secret attic area, Jancy came up with another "game" story.

"We're going to play a kind of hide-and-seek game," she told Trixie and Buddy. "But the best part is that nobody knows when we're going to start playing. That part will be a surprise. The game starts all of a sudden when somebody says, 'Here we go,' and then everybody has to run through Aunt Fiona's bedroom and into her closet and through that little door, and shut the door and be very quiet."

"Can I say it?" Trixie asked. "Can I be the one to say, 'Here we go'?"

"No," Jancy said. "It has to be William or Aunt Fiona or me."

Trixie began to whimper. "But I want to say it. Why can't I be the one to say it?"

"Because that's the way the rules are." Jancy was sounding exasperated. "The rules say only people who are older than ten get to decide when to say, 'Here we go.' Okay?"

Trixie didn't look happy, but she shrugged and said, "Okay then. I won't say it right away. But I get to have my turn as soon as I'm ten. Okay?"

So they had to promise her she could be the one to say, "Here we go" when she got to be ten years old, and then they all went down to the kitchen and started a practice run. Aunt Fiona said, "Here we go," and all four of them ran up the stairs, down the hall, through the bedroom and closet, climbed through the little door, squeezed into the secret attic, and closed the door behind them. Trixie and Buddy loved it. In fact, they wanted to keep doing it over and over. But after they'd done it three or four times, they finally agreed to go back to trying to learn how to do pick-up sticks.

The next day and the one after that, Auntie seemed to be fairly relaxed. Either that, or she was really good at pretending she was. She went right ahead doing everyday things in a calm, ordinary way. Like making plans about what would happen when school started. As if it really was for certain that the four of them would still be there.

"I've talked to a friend of mine who says she'd be glad to take care of Buddy while I'm teaching," she told Jancy. "And you and Trixie can ride to school with me, if you don't mind going a little early. We'll drop William off at the junior high and then go right on to Gold Beach Elementary."

They didn't mind. William thought that riding to school every day in Aunt Fiona's car, instead of having to ride the school bus, would be a nice change. He was beginning to really look forward to the first day of school. To the time when he could stop hanging around the house all day, listening for suspicious noises and running to look out the front windows every time he heard a strange sound.

Where Aunt Fiona lived, at the end of Eleanor Street, there wasn't much traffic, and that seemed to make the problem worse. The windows had to be kept open in the hot summer weather, so every time a car did go by, it was pretty noticeable. Particularly if the car had a noisy engine, like the old wrecks the Baggetts usually owned.

William found himself listening and watching pretty constantly. Watching to be sure the kids hadn't left any clothes or toys lying around, as well as listening for cars. Particularly listening for a noisy car that sounded as if it was getting ready to stop. Two or three times a day a thumping motor or a squeal of brakes would send him racing to the window, only to catch sight of the offending car and see that it wasn't full of Baggetts—and walk away, reminding himself to start breathing again.

Two more days went by like that, but then, right after lunch on a gray, muggy Thursday, William was in the living room reading one of Aunt Fiona's books, when there was a chugging, coughing roar that came from just outside the house. And when he ran to the window, the first thing he saw was Rudy Baggett climbing out of a big, rusty car. Climbing out, slamming the door behind him, and joining Big and Little Ed, who were already headed for Aunt Fiona's front door.

A split second of stunned disbelief, and William was swinging into action. Calling, "Here we go," he ran into the kitchen, where Trixie and Buddy had made a playhouse by hanging a sheet over a card table. Still saying, "Here we go, here we go" in a loud whisper, he stuffed the sheet into a drawer, grabbed Trixie and Buddy's hands, and headed for the stairs. After the first startled-stiff minute the kids got their act together, and by the time they'd reached the top of the stairs they were both squealing, "Here we go." And Jancy was right behind them, with her arms full of things they'd left lying around the house. Things like an old baby doll and a bunch of pick-up sticks.

By the time they'd reached Aunt Fiona's bedroom the doorbell had started to ring, one loud, demanding jangle after another.

"Hush. Stop yelling. Be quiet," William was whispering as he pushed the two little kids headfirst through the little opening in the closet wall and climbed in over them. And a few seconds later Jancy was there too.

Pulling the door closed, William whispered, "Everybody be very quiet."

And then it was absolutely quiet, and very dark. The silence lasted for a minute or two before Trixie asked, "Is whispering against the rules?"

William and Jancy said, "Shh!" in unison.

Minutes passed. Except for the soft whisper of hushed breathing, no sound at all. But then suddenly there were footsteps, soft and far away at first, but quickly getting louder and nearer. And voices. Loud, demanding voices that faded briefly and came back again. More footsteps and even louder voices, louder and clearer.

William's heart was already pounding against his ribs when he heard a gasp, and then another. And then Trixie was saying in a whispery whimper, "Big Ed? Is that Big Ed, William?"

Pressing his lips against Trixie's ear, William barely breathed, "Yes, it is. Be still."

Trixie stopped whimpering. Stopped so immediately and completely that for a moment William wondered if she'd stopped breathing, but when he put his ear against her skinny little chest, he could hear the rapid pounding of her heart.

And then, very near their hiding place, a different Baggetty voice was shouting. Shouting loudly enough for even people shut away in an attic hideout to hear and understand the words. "Look here, Pop. Look what Little Ed found downstairs. They're here, all right. They got to be."

A softer voice followed. Softer and very familiar. Aunt Fiona was saying something only partly under-standable, but clearly pleading, begging. "Please. Please. Just go away." A moment more of unintelligible pleading. And then, louder, "Don't. Please don't. Stop it. You're hurting me."

And suddenly, before anyone could stop him, Buddy was shouting, "No. No. You stop that. Don't hurt Auntie." And Buddy was shoving William's hands away and struggling to push open the attic door and wiggle his way out into the closet. By the time William was able to follow him, Buddy had run to Aunt Fiona, and with his back against her legs and both his clenched fists held out in front of him, he was threatening the Baggetts. Threatening to take on the three big men who were staring at him in disbelief—staring and then convulsing in loud roars of laughter.

The laughter didn't last long. And it didn't take much longer for the Baggetts to find their hiding place and pull the rest of them out. To find them and drag them, with Trixie crying hysterically and Buddy yelling and William and Jancy shocked into frozen silence, down the stairs to the front door.

There was a brief pause there, when Big Ed ordered

William to go back and get their clothing. "All of it," he yelled. "I'm not going to get stuck with buying you good-for-nothing tramps a bunch of new school clothes. Now get going. Rudy, go with him and see that he does as he's told. Just some stuff for them to wear. Nothing else. Ya hear me?"

"You heard him. Just your duds," Rudy repeated when William tried to add **Doubleday's Complete Works** to his jam-packed knapsack. "Nothing else."

And then they drove away—away from Gold Beach and 971 Eleanor Street, leaving Aunt Fiona standing on the front porch with her hand pressed against her cheek and tears running down her face.

It didn't take nearly as long to go the one hundred miles between Gold Beach and Crownfield in the Baggetts' car as it had on the bus, but to William it seemed like forever. A forever of having to try to answer the questions Big Ed shouted back at him from the driver's seat. Questions like, "What kind of excuse you got for running away from your home and family—and taking those two helpless little tykes with you? Just making sure they're going to turn into the same kind of sneaking lying tramp you are, and always have been?" And a little later, "And how you going to explain where you got the money to take all four of you all that way on the bus? Tell me that. Bet I know now what's been happening to the hard-earned cash me and your brothers been missing lately." At first William tried to answer and explain, but it was no use.

In between the questioning sessions William could only listen to Trixie's soft sobs and Buddy's constant questions. Questions about where they were going and why. "Why can't we stay at Auntie's? Why, Willum? Why?"

It was pretty obvious that Big Ed, and the rest of the Baggetts as well, blamed William for the escape attempt, and they meant to see that he never tried it again. By the time they'd been back at the farmhouse for three or four days, William had been beaten hard with Big Ed's long leather belt, and slapped around more times than he could count. Jancy got whipped too, but just with a switch, and not quite as long and hard. And in between the beatings, they both were carefully watched and spied on by one or another Baggett. Even by Babe, who ordinarily didn't do anything except comb her hair and put on makeup.

They were watched so closely that it wasn't until three or four days later, on a particularly hot afternoon when everyone seemed to be napping, that William and Jancy finally managed to get to their old meeting place in the moldy hayloft. They had a lot of things to talk about. The first and most important was Trixie.

"I'm really worried about her," Jancy said as soon as they reached their hiding place. "She's so quiet. It's just not like her at all. She's been that way ever since he made her stand there and watch while he beat you with his belt. I tried to take her away, but he wouldn't let me."

"I know. I saw her," William said. With his hands over his face to protect it from the whip, as well as hide his tears, he hadn't seen much. But he did catch a glimpse of Trixie's pale, frightened face and heard big Ed yelling at Jancy, "Stay right there and watch. Both of you. You'll get it too, missy, if you ever try to run out on me again."

William sneezed, sniffed, and swallowed hard before he could go on, "But I've hardly seen her since then. Where has she been? Doesn't she ever come out of your room?"

"She never wants to. Not even to eat." Jancy's large eyes were full of tears. "She wants me to stay there with her, and if I have to go out for even a few minutes, she hides herself. When I come back, she's usually in the closet or under the bed. That's probably where she is right now."

William felt mostly anger, but as he pictured a silent, frightened Trixie trying to find a way to hide herself, his eyes got involved too. He had to blink hard and shake his head before he managed to say, "But Buddy? He doesn't seem to be doing so bad."

"That dumb kid," Jancy said. "If he'd just kept quiet we might still be at Aunt Fiona's right this minute."

"Oh, I don't know," William said. "I don't think it would have made any difference. You know when we crawled out they were all there in Aunt Fiona's room, and Rudy was holding that Raggedy Ann doll. The one that Trixie was playing with that morning. He must have found it lying around the house. So that kind of gave it away. They probably would have threatened Aunt Fiona until she told. Maybe even twisted her arm or something. I think Big Ed had already started to do something like that when Buddy started yelling."

"Yeah. Well, maybe you're right." Jancy sighed. She thought a minute longer before she went on, "Those lousy crumb bums might have hurt her real bad if she wouldn't tell, and if Buddy hadn't started yelling at them."

"I know, and besides . . ." William had to stop to sneeze again before he went on. As if things weren't bad enough at the Baggetts, there was always the hay fever. "You know what?" he finally managed to say. "I think they must have kind of liked what he did. I know they laughed at him, but . . . but maybe his trying to stand up to them that way made things a little better for him. Don't you think they've gone a little easier on him since we got back? They don't even tease him as much as they used to."

"Yeah?" Jancy was beginning to nod. "I guess he *hasn't* had it quite as bad as the rest of us. I thought that was just because he's the littlest."

"That might be part of it," William said. "Sort of. Because he's little—but mostly because he's . . . tough." He paused, and then went on. "When a little kid like Buddy is ready to take on three full-grown guys, that's something that might get anybody's attention, even a Baggett. I think that might be why they've laid off him a little."

"Yeah, well, maybe," Jancy said. She shook her head, looking thoughtful. "But that scares me even more."

"Why's that?" William was puzzled.

"Well, you know how much Buddy likes folks to like him? If he starts thinking those Baggetts like him, he just might start liking them back." Jancy's still tear-wet eyes widened as if in fright. "He might even start wanting to act like them."

William saw what she meant. Buddy wasn't exactly perfect as it was, but a Buddy who was trying to grow up to be another Rudy or Little Ed could be a lot worse. It was a troublesome thought. But what to do about it? Nothing came to mind immediately, and it was time to cut things short and hurry back to the house before someone woke up and started looking for them.

So time went by, and after those first few terrible days, most things had gone back to being nearly the same as before they ran away—no better, but not a whole lot worse. Trixie had begun to come out of her hiding places (but only if Jancy stayed right beside her), Gertie's cooking was as bad as ever, and the big Baggett kids' favorite form of indoor sport was still tormenting anyone smaller than they were.

But in some very important ways, things were worse than ever for William. First off was the fact that without his Getaway Fund, there wasn't even that exciting "someday" to look forward to. No more daydreams about Hollywood or Broadway in the not-too-distant future.

And in the meantime, there wasn't even his journal or 𝔇oubleday's ℭomplete 𝔚orks to fall back on. Not anymore. It helped a little to remind himself that Aunt Fiona would keep them safe, and maybe someday he could get them back. But that was in a future so out of reach he could barely dream about it.

So there he was, back in the hot, smelly attic with less to look forward to and a lot more to worry about. The only thing left that helped a little, when he was trying to get to sleep, was reminding himself of the fact that August was almost over and the school year was about to start. And of course, the best thing about school was that he'd be taking English from Miss Scott. At the moment, the possibility of being in Miss Scott's class again was just about the only good thing the future was likely to bring.

Of course, there was still the real possibility that Big Ed wouldn't let him and Jancy go to school anymore for fear that once out of sight, they'd just up and run away again. But maybe not. Since he'd already had so many run-ins with Crownfield's truant officers, perhaps Big Ed wouldn't have the nerve to keep two more of his kids out of school.

So that was how things stood when, a day or two after the beginning of September, the Baggetts' social worker came to make one of her usual visits. Mrs. Montgomery was a tall, worried-looking woman, with lots of grayish hair wrapped around her head in a thick braid. William had always been glad to see her. Her visits had never seemed to change anything for the better, but at least for the short time she was right there in the house, there was a lot less yelling and punching.

William was the one who went to the door when she knocked, but Big Ed got up off the couch and limped over as soon as he saw who it was. Limped a lot worse than usual, to show Mrs. Montgomery how bad off he was. So crippled he couldn't even drive a dump truck, if she still had a job like that to offer him. And also, as always, he made all his kids line up and be counted so the social worker would know what a lot of President Roosevelt's relief money the family needed. He even made Jancy drag poor little stiff-faced, tearful Trixie out to stand in line with the rest of them.

Watching the social worker that day, William got the feeling that she didn't actually believe everything Big Ed was telling her, and she would have liked to say so, only she didn't quite dare. She looked particularly suspicious when Big Ed said, "And they'll all be starting school again in a few days. All of them except the baby there, and Ed Junior and Rudy, over at the other end of the line. But my little cutie, Trixie—what you crying about, Trixie, this nice lady isn't goin' to hurt you—she'll be starting school too this year. And that makes seven of them. And believe you me, seeing to it that seven kids gets a good education, that takes a lot out of my wallet. You know, all them clothes and books and lunches."

At that point the social worker started to say, "Well, I have checked into last year's attendance records at the high school and . . ."

But then Big Ed's eyebrows started to twitch, and he began to throw his arms around and yell. Stomping around the room, he cussed and yelled stuff about how bad the schools were, and how they never bothered to check up on whether people were there or not—and how the stupid teachers marked kids absent when they really weren't. And on and on and on. Mrs. Montgomery got very quiet. And it wasn't long before she gathered up her papers and went away. And everybody went right back to whatever they'd been doing, or not doing, before she showed up.

But then, only two days later, there was another loud knock on the Baggetts' front door. Loud and long lasting. This time Big Ed was busy drinking beer and beating Little Ed in a game of checkers, while two or three of the other Baggetts were busy standing around watching the game and cheering every time Big Ed took one of

Little Ed's pieces. Baggett kids, even the large ones, knew better than to cheer for anybody who was trying to beat Big Ed.

So Big Ed yelled at William to answer the door. "Get going, Willy," he bellowed. "Answer the goddamn door." William got to the door as fast as he could, but when he snatched it open, he just stood there staring, shocked into frozen silence.

What he seemed to be seeing was a whole crowd of people. Some of them carefully balanced on the sloping, broken-down veranda, and some others down on the path. To William's absolute astonishment, one of them was Mrs. Montgomery, the social worker, and next to her was a broad-shouldered guy wearing a police uniform. Behind them were two important and confident-looking people carrying briefcases—a man and a woman he'd never seen before. And down at the bottom of the steps were Miss Scott and Aunt Fiona.

How did it happen? It took a long time to put all the facts together and understand how one thing led to another, then another, and eventually caused those six people to show up on the Baggetts' front porch. A long time for William and Jancy to learn exactly what had started it, and what happened next, and where it had gone from there.

Actually, unlikely as it might seem, the very first step that eventually led to the arrival of those six people on the Baggetts' veranda was taken by Clarice Ogden on that same Saturday morning when the four runaway Baggetts sneaked out of her basement and caught the bus to Reedly. On that morning, after her parents finally left for their Chamber of Commerce lunch meeting around eleven o'clock, Clarice rushed down to the basement, only to find that the four Baggetts and all their belongings had disappeared. Right at first, she had been surprised and disappointed, and sad—and then *angry*.

It was right then, while she was still down in the

basement looking around and remembering how exciting it had been and how well she'd arranged everything, that she found something very interesting. On the counter in the little kitchen she found the note Jancy had left behind on purpose. The note that said she and William had borrowed one of the oldest suitcases, and that they would return it as soon as possible.

That was all the information in the note, but right there under it, kind of crinkled up with it, was an empty envelope. A wrinkled, beat-up-looking envelope with a return address up in the corner that said, in adult-type handwriting, "Fiona Hardison, 971 Eleanor Street, Gold Beach, California." That was when Clarice remembered that William and Jancy had said they were headed for Gold Beach, and she also remembered that William had said that Hardison was his mother's last name before she became a Baggett.

Clarice, a Sherlock Holmes fan, had stared at the envelope for a long time before she said to Ursa, "Aha! I'm making a brilliant deduction, Watson." Ursa sat up, cocked his head, and sniffed the envelope. "See that," Clarice went on, "that, right there, is obviously their aunt's address, and my superior detecting skill is telling me where that sneaky, ungrateful bunch of Baggetts are right this minute."

Finding Jancy's lost envelope was an important part of the final outcome, because of what Clarice decided to do then, which was to write a letter. A letter to William in Gold Beach, and to Jancy, too, of course. It turned out to be a long letter, in which she scolded him/them for leaving without telling her they were going, after all she'd done for them. After she'd hid them for such a long time and cooked all those wonderful meals for them. The letter started out just a little bit angry, but then it got *angrier*, and toward the end it said,

> *So I guess it's a good thing you cleared out when you did, because the rest of your awful family, that disgusting Baggett mob, is in big trouble again. Serious trouble, things like drunk driving.*

And then in even larger and darker letters,

Not to mention bank robbery and murder.

It took her quite a few days to finish the letter, especially the part she had to kind of make up as she went along—the part, that is, about the robbery and the murder. At first the murder victim was a bank employee, and then she decided to change it to a policeman. By the time Clarice's long letter was finally finished and arrived at Aunt Fiona's, the Baggetts had been there, and the kids were gone—stolen away and taken back to the farmhouse on the Old Westbrook Highway. And since Aunt Fiona was sure William would never get the letter if she forwarded it to the Baggetts, she decided to read it herself. After she did, she felt she had to call the mysterious Clarice Ogden, who had conveniently included her phone number.

What Fiona Hardison meant to do was simply call the Ogden family and thank them for being so good to her nieces and nephews by trying to help them escape from the Baggetts. And also, of course, to ask for more information about the recent crimes those other Baggetts had committed, which distressed but didn't surprise her, and of which she hadn't been aware. Crimes that now that she knew about them, increased the deep concern she was feeling for her nieces and nephews.

But Aunt Fiona happened to call on a Saturday, and it was Mr. Ogden, the lawyer and almost famous judge, who answered the phone. And since the only thing William and Jancy had told Aunt Fiona about their stay in Crownfield was that "a friend had let them hide in their basement," she didn't realize that the friend's parents hadn't known anything about it. So she thanked him for allowing the four runaway Baggett kids to be hidden and protected on his property. "The children arrived here safely, and they were here with me until . . . ," she told Mr. Ogden in a shaky, tearful voice that stammered to a stop and then managed to go on. "Until the day before yesterday, but then their father showed up and took them away."

It took a while for her to steady her voice enough to ask about the recent murder, and who it was the Baggetts had killed.

At first Mr. Ogden had been absolutely astonished, and not at all sure Fiona Hardison was in her right mind. He did try to calm the poor woman by telling her he hadn't heard anything about a murder. But then, as soon as he hung up the phone, he went up to Clarice's room and knocked on the door.

His first words to Clarice were, "Do you know anything about a Fiona Hardison who lives in Gold Beach, and why she would think we've been hiding some runaway children on our property?"

Clarice stared at her father with her mouth hanging open for a long moment, before she closed it, swallowed hard, and began, "Well, yes, I do know who she is. She's related to some of the Baggetts. Like an aunt or something, and . . . and . . ." She stopped, squared her chin, and went on. "We did have some Baggetts—some little ones, anyway—hiding in our basement." She swallowed again, raised her chin, and said, "I did it, and I'm glad."

Encouraged by the fact that the expression on her father's face was closer to astonishment than anger, she went on. "The Baggetts who ran away are the four youngest ones. The ones who had a different mother, and they were running away because . . ." She paused, caught her breath, and went on. "Because those other Baggetts were starving and beating and torturing them. They were on their way to their aunt's house when I met them, but the other Baggetts were about to catch up with them, so I hid them in our basement." At that point she lifted her chin up even higher and said, "I probably saved their lives, and I'm glad I did and I'd do it again if I could."

At that point Mr. Ogden said he wanted Clarice's mother to hear this, so they went downstairs and Clarice told her story all over again, adding some new, exciting details. Details about how she'd been out with Ursa early in the morning when she found the little kids hiding in the bushes because a huge gang of Baggetts carrying whips and guns had just started down Gardenia Street. And some other facts and figures like how much of her allowance money and her free time she'd spent feeding and taking care of the runaways. An only slightly embellished account that wound up, "And I'd have told you about it right away, except I was afraid you might insist on turning those poor little kids over to the authorities, who would probably have given them right back to their awful father." At that point Clarice managed to produce a few real tears, and her parents began to comfort her and tell her she'd done what she did for good reasons, and she wouldn't be punished for it.

It was after Clarice confessed to her parents that the really surprising thing occurred—at least it certainly surprised Clarice. It turned out that her parents were *not* angry at her for having hidden the four runaway Baggett kids in their basement. In fact, they seemed rather pleased about what she had done—and proud of her for having pulled it all off in such a clever and well-organized way.

That part of her confession went smoothly, but later, when her father asked her why this Miss Hardison seemed to think that some of the Baggetts had recently committed a murder, she didn't do quite as well. But finally she had to admit that she did exaggerate just a tiny bit in the letter she'd sent to the runaways after they left for Gold Beach. And when her mother asked her why, she said she did it so those poor little Baggetts would realize how important it was for them to stay in Gold Beach and never come back to Crownfield and their awful relatives.

It wasn't until then that Clarice's father remembered to tell her that, according to their aunt, the Baggetts had already arrived and the children had been taken away. And that was when Clarice absolutely insisted that they, the three of them, had to do something about it. She was the one who started it, but it was her mother, Adele Ogden, attorney, who decided, when she heard that one of the runaways was the boy who'd played the part of Ariel, that she should get in touch with her friend Julia Scott and tell her about it.

When she did, she asked Miss Scott if she knew that the four youngest Baggett kids, including that talented boy who'd played Ariel, had recently run away from their dreadful family and that they had gone to live with an aunt in Gold Beach. But then the Baggetts had found them and forcibly taken them back to that crumbling farmhouse out on Old Westbrook Road.

Miss Scott had answered that she hadn't known, but that she thought William was a great kid, with an amazing amount of talent, and that she would be willing to help in whatever way she could. She was the one who suggested that a trip to Gold Beach to meet with the children's aunt might be the first step. And so it was. The four of them—Miss Scott, Jefferson and Adele Ogden, and Clarice, too—had driven all the way to Gold Beach for a conference with Aunt Fiona.

That was when Fiona Hardison told them about how she had taken care of the two youngest Baggetts for two whole years right after their mother died, and then had them snatched away from her. And, more recently, how threatening and violent Big Ed and two other enormous Baggetts had been when they came to her house and took all four of the children away. When they heard that, the Ogdens and Miss Scott were even more determined to arrange for the children to be returned to their aunt.

During their conference in Gold Beach, the two Ogden lawyers told Aunt Fiona that it was usually very difficult to take children away from their biological parents or, as in this case, biological father and stepmother, no matter how bad they had been at parenting. But then the Ogden's told her that they might have a case if any or all of the following things were true:

1. If the parent had a reputation as a violent person.
2. If there was proof that the children had been mistreated or poorly fed.
3. If the parent had misled the welfare people who were assigned to his case.
4. If the children would testify that they preferred to live with a reliable friend or relative who had agreed to care for them.

And Fiona Hardison's answers had been:

1. Yes, he has.
2. Yes, there is.
3. Yes, I'm sure he has.
4. Yes, I'm sure they would.

"Well then, my dear," Adele Ogden, attorney, had said, patting Aunt Fiona on the shoulder, "I'm sure we can win the case in any court of law."

And Jefferson Ogden, attorney, added, "That may not even be necessary, Adele. I have a feeling that if we give Mr. Baggett a realistic picture of where the trial was almost certain to wind up, he'll come around to our way of thinking about the future of his four youngest children."

As soon as they returned to Crownfield, they contacted Mrs. Montgomery, the social worker, to gather some more information that might be useful. Things about how Big Ed and most of his older offspring had lots of unpaid traffic tickets and fines for driving under the influence and driving without a license. And how the four Baggett teenagers who were supposed to be going to Crownfield High School almost never attended. And when they asked Mrs. Montgomery if she would like to be present when they confronted Ed Baggett, she said she would, but she'd feel better about it if her policeman husband could be there too, because she had always found Mr. Ed Baggett to be rather intimidating.

So they arranged a date when all six of them—the two Ogden lawyers, Aunt Fiona, Miss Scott, and Mrs. Montgomery, along with her husband, Sergeant Montgomery—could show up unannounced on the Baggetts' front steps. So they did. And that was when William went to the door and let them in.

By the time the visit was over, Big Ed was stomping around the farmhouse, yelling and roaring, even forgetting to limp, and finally shouting at William and Jancy, "Get out, and take those little brats with you, and

I hope I never see any of you again, long as I live."

Sometime later William wished he'd yelled back. Wished he had, for once in his life, yelled back at Big Ed. But of course he didn't. Right then, while it was all happening, the only thing that filled William's mind was a rising tide of hope that made him just stand there grinning while Big Ed raged and swore. The last thing William S. did as a Baggett was to hold the door open for his little sisters and brother and their six rescuers, and close it firmly behind him.

So that was that, and only a day later they were back with Aunt Fiona in Gold Beach. Back in the nice old house on Eleanor Street, and this time no longer needing to listen constantly for the threatening sound of a noisy car or the stomp of heavy boots on the front steps. Instead there were only minor problems connected with getting everyone ready for the start of a new school year. William would be going to Gold Beach Junior High. Jancy and Trixie would be in sixth and first grade, at the same elementary school where Aunt Fiona taught fourth grade. And a neighbor on Eleanor Street, who had preschool kids of her own, would be able to take care of Buddy during the school day.

Then came William's thirteenth birthday, and Aunt Fiona baked a cake and, as a birthday present, gave him some extra money to buy school clothes. That was on the Friday before school started, and after they all sang happy birthday and ate the cake, William got ready to go shopping. Aunt Fiona was planning to take Jancy and the little kids to a dress sale at JCPenney, but Buddy refused to go.

"I don't suppose to go shoppin' with girls," he kept saying. "I want to go shoppin' with Willum." So William wound up having to take Buddy with him. They went to Montgomery Ward, and William got some new pants and shoes, and two pretty snazzy new shirts. And Buddy wasn't too much trouble. Except for sticking his tongue out at all the plaster mannequins and trying to push the buttons on a couple of cash registers, he behaved pretty well.

On their way home, when they happened to go past a pet shop, Buddy tugged on the back of William's new shirt and said, "Let's go in there. See the picture? They got aminals in there."

"Animals," William corrected. "*Animals!* Okay, but just for a minute. It's almost time for dinner." So they went in and looked at some bright-colored fish in an aquarium and two noisy parrots—and then, at the back of the shop, two cages full of guinea pigs.

When William looked at the blob-shaped little animals, it brought back a bunch of Baggett memories, including Jancy's tear-wet face that terrible day when Sweetie Pie went down the drain. And that, of course, reminded him of the part Buddy had played in the whole tragedy. William once again found himself thinking that even a four-year-old ought to have enough brains to know you shouldn't try to bathe a guinea pig, or anything else, in a toilet. It really had been mostly Buddy's fault, even if the twins had put him up to it. Dumb kid!

Grabbing Buddy's arm, he gave him an angry jerk toward the front of the shop. "Okay, kid. I've seen enough. Let's get out of here," he said.

But Buddy wouldn't come. Planting his feet firmly, he pulled away and said, "No. Not yet. Not till I buy a gunny pig for Jancy."

William stared in surprise, and then started to grin. "Real good idea, Buddy boy," he said. "Good thinking. Except you don't have any money."

"I know," Buddy agreed, "but you do."

"Not enough," William told him. But he looked through his pockets anyway and found he did have a little leftover change. When he told the pet shop owner how much money they had, it turned out that guinea pigs were on sale that day. On sale, the owner said, because he'd recently had some unexpected guinea pig litters, and besides, on the first week of September most of his regular customers were too busy shopping for school things to think about buying a new pet. So a few minutes later, William and Buddy were on their way home again, carrying a dusty-orange-colored guinea pig in a cardboard box with breathing holes.

They were nearly home when Buddy said, "What's his name? What's the new gunny pig's name, Willum?"

William thought for a minute before he said, "How about Act Two?"

"Achoo?" Buddy asked.

"No," William said. "Act Two. His name could be Sweetie Pie, Act Two."

Actually, Jancy decided to name her new guinea pig Pumpkin because of his shape and color. But when William told her how Buddy had insisted on buying it, she told Buddy her guinea pig was going to have a middle name too. "His name is going to be Pumpkin Buddy Hardison," she told him. "Would that be all right?"

Buddy said it would.

So, just like before, things were real good at Aunt Fiona's—almost everything. The only downer for William was the fact that there was no Miss Scott at Gold Beach Junior High. In fact, there wasn't even a drama department at the small high school where he would be going the following year.

Oh well, William kept telling himself, *don't think about it. You can't have everything.* Not that that kind of thinking helped very much. Nothing did, really. Not even reminding himself that as soon as school got under way he'd be too busy to wonder about what 𝔖𝔥𝔞𝔨𝔢𝔰𝔭𝔢𝔞𝔯𝔢 play Miss Scott was working on this year, and whether there might have been a role in it for him. A 𝔖𝔥𝔞𝔨𝔢𝔰𝔭𝔢𝔞𝔯𝔢𝔞𝔫 role for William 𝔖. Hardison, which would soon be his real name, as well as his future stage name. Just as soon as

Aunt Fiona, with the Ogdens' help, finished the official change-of-name papers for all four of the kids.

But the very next day, the Saturday before school started, he got a letter from Miss Julia Scott. The first part of the letter was just kind of chatty. She wrote about how she was going to miss having him in her eighth-grade English class, and what books she hoped he'd be assigned to read. But then she got to the important part.

It seemed that Miss Scott had been asked to be a director at a kind of drama camp someplace near San Francisco next summer, and that the play she would be directing was going to be **A Midsummer Night's Dream.** *"And I so much want you to try out for the role of Puck. Knowing you as I do, I'm certain that you'll get the part,"* her letter said.

> *Your natural ability to clown around and really lose yourself in a role, as well as your size and stature, make you perfect for the role. I'm sure your aunt will agree to let you spend part of the summer away from home. Living quarters are being provided for the cast, and I can arrange for your transportation.*

William read the letter on his way upstairs, and when he'd finished reading he yelled, "Wahoo!" and ran the rest of the way, waving the letter over his head.

Dashing down the hall, he almost ran over Jancy, who was just coming out of her room. As he started reading the letter to her Trixie showed up and, a few minutes later, Buddy. "Why was Willum going, 'Wahoo'?" Buddy asked Trixie.

"About a play," Trixie said. "About a play he's going to do."

"Oh," Buddy said. "Do we get to play too?"

"No, I don't think so," Trixie was saying as they went on down the hall. "It's not that kind of play. I think maybe it's another thing you can't do till you're ten years old."

William read the letter over and over again for most of the afternoon.

So it was all arranged. Aunt Fiona had no objections. In fact, she said she thought it was a wonderful opportunity for William to develop his natural God-given talents.

So that left only the business of getting through the school year with his usual good grades, and in the meantime practicing the role of Puck as often as possible.

He started right away, reciting Puck's lines for the kids as well as Aunt Fiona, and thinking up ways to prance and pose while he was putting the magic love potion on people's eyes. As always, he had a very appreciative audience. Jancy said she thought he was going to be an even better Puck than he was an Ariel.

80·CB

It was only a few days after school started, when another letter arrived at 971 Eleanor Street. The letter was addressed to William S. Hardison, and the return address was *"Clarice Ogden, 1036 Gardenia Ave., Crownfield, California."*

William was surprised and, well, pretty curious. Jancy, who had been looking over his shoulder when he got the letter out of Aunt Fiona's mailbox, seemed to be even more so.

"Hey," she shrieked. "Look at that. It's from Clarice. I bet it's a love letter."

William ignored her. Turning away, trying to keep her from reading over his shoulder, he tore open the envelope and began to read.

"Dear William," the letter began.

"Dear William!" Jancy was squealing. Clasping her hands under her chin and looking soulful, she kept repeating, "My dear, dear, William."

"Get out of here, you lamebrain," William told her. "That doesn't mean anything. That's the way all letters start. 'Dear whoever.'" Sure enough, the first few lines were just the usual how-are-you stuff. But then came:

> *I saw Julia Scott last night. She came to a party*
> *at our house, and she was telling us about how*
> *she is going to be the director for a Shakespeare*

festival in the Bay Area next summer. <u>And</u> that she is going to ask you to try out for the role of Puck in <u>A Midsummer Night's Dream</u>. I know you'll get the part. After all, Miss Scott will probably be doing the casting. How could you lose? Ha! Ha!

But now comes my big news. My folks have to do a lot of traveling next summer, and they'd already asked Miss Scott if I could stay with her while they are away. And last night she told my folks that it would still be all right for me to stay with her if I didn't mind going to the Shakespeare thing. So maybe I'm going to be in the play too. Well, maybe not actually acting in it, but Miss Scott says that if I don't get an actual part in the play, I can probably get a job in the costume room or else doing makeup. I'm very good at making people up.

William grinned, thinking that was for sure. He had good reason to know that Clarice Ogden had been pretty good at making up a bunch of police cars and posters, not to mention a Baggett murder victim.

The letter went on for several paragraphs after that. One whole section was about how she had been getting along with her parents much better recently.

I guess it wasn't so much that they wished they didn't have me, like I used to think. It's just that lawyers have to keep their minds so full of all those legal facts that they can't be expected to spend much time thinking about less important stuff—like their only child. But now that I'm old enough to think up a lot of good ways to help them remember, we seem to be getting along better.

Then there was another paragraph about how she was sorry she'd been so angry at William when he took the little kids and went off without even telling her he was going. But she had completely forgiven him now, and she knew that they were going to go on being "<u>very close friends</u>."

Not too bad, except for the underlining. But Jancy, who was back to reading over his shoulder, again began to squeal.

"*Very close friends.*" She giggled. "Very, very friendly."

But then Trixie, who had suddenly appeared on the veranda, said, "Who's friendly, Jancy?"

"Clarice and William," Jancy told Trixie. "Didn't you know?" She rolled her eyes and clasped her hands over her heart. "Clarice is in love with William."

"And Jancy is nuts," William said. And then to Jancy,

"You were the one who said that if Clarice was crazy about anyone, it was Ariel, not me. Right?"

Jancy was still snickering. "Oh, sure," she said. "But if she was crazy about Ariel, how do you think she's going to feel about Puck?"

"I don't know," William said. "I don't know about that." He shrugged and gave Jancy a sheepish halfway grin. "But it looks to me like . . ."

"Like what?" Jancy insisted.

He paused, trying to think of a **Shakespeare** quote that said what he had in mind. Of course there was, "**All's well that ends well.**" That would be a good quote, he felt sure, to describe what William **S.** Hardison's thirteenth summer was going to be like—at least for the most part. For the terribly exciting part in which he would have a great time being Puck in an important production of **A Midsummer Night's Dream**. But as for a summer spent with Clarice Ogden, more or less in the same scene . . .

"Who knows?" he told Jancy. "I guess we'll just have to wait and see."

"Wait for what?" Jancy demanded.

William threw out his arms, bent one knee, and did a fancy final curtain bow. "For the end of the play," he said.